D1534697

Copyright ©2022 by Neet Frazier-Diggs

Hurting People Hurt People, But God Heals All Wounds

ISBN: 979-8-218-07076-2

Written by: Neet Frazier- Diggs

Self-Published by: Curls & Coils Literary Solutions

Dedication

To my mother, Eve S. Demby, who chose not to abort me, even when people told you that you were too young to keep me. We grew up together and although I know it wasn't easy, I have seen you remain strong through all of your adversities. I thank you for choosing me!

~~~~~~

To my loving daughter, MaLeah Diggs, who was perfect for me. God knew exactly what I needed to continue this race. Your smile, your temperament, your personality, you are beautiful inside and out and it is a privilege to be your mom. I look forward to seeing where God will take you on your journey. You make me proud, I love watching you grow and I love you with all my heart!

~~~~~~

To my sisters, Evette and Eleicia, who have always supported me; I appreciate you.

~~~~~~

I'm blessed to still have the matriarchs of my family: my Aunt Clara Miller; and my two Grandfathers: James Brown and Calvin Frazier. They are all over 80 and still lovingly a part of my life.

~~~~~~

To the Village of family and friends, I can't thank you enough!

~~~~~~

Thank you to Chaundra Scott, for allowing God to use you to push me, motivate me and keep me on task; but most of all for your patience in helping me to get this out to the world.

Acknowledgements

- To my PIPSIL, my friend, the late Elder Denise Diggs. It still took me five more years after you were gone to complete, but I'm grateful. For all the times you let me talk about this book that I was writing even when only a few words were on the paper. Thank you for the many nights you listened and encouraged me to do it. Well I finally did it! To God Be the Glory!

In Loving Memory of:
- My dear Grand, the late Patricia A. Pringle, life was so much easier when you were here. I'm so grateful for everything that you poured into my life. Your faithfulness to God and the life that you lived were examples to walk in faith no matter what. It has helped me to continue on this path and to stay committed to the process. I miss you so much!
- My grandmother, the late Julia Williams, I remember when I became your granddaughter, although it was through marriage, I was the happiest little girl in the world. I couldn't believe that you were now someone that I could call family. Your inspiration, your tenacity and your firmness taught me to be strong and to never give up. I will always appreciate our talks and even the quiet moments. Although I didn't know it then, those Saturdays when wrestling was on and I couldn't move, taught me to be still and know that God is real.
- My godmother, the late Deborah Jean Johnson. You came into my life when I was a young teenager, confused and filled with turmoil. I'm pretty sure God sent you to help me to stay alive during those difficult times. You taught me so many things in life and I only pray that I am able to pour back into someone else at least half of what you poured into me. You taught me that life was worth living and no matter what was going on, I always knew I could come to you and not be judged, no matter how crazy the thoughts were. I thank you.
- My dear husband, the late Michael Diggs, losing you taught me that life is precious and we must cherish those that we love every day. I am grateful for the times we had to share and thank God that He allowed us to share not only friendship, but also a love to the end.

Disclaimer

The stories in this book are based on personal experiences and offer limited professional knowledge. Enclosed perspectives are from observations only. This information should not be used as clinical advice. For more information or concerns, please seek assistance from a licensed counseling professional.

Hurting People Hurt People, But God Heals ALL Wounds

Short Stories With Long-Lasting Effects

By Neet Frazier-Diggs

Table Of Contents

Foreword

*"**Just maybe, but what if**?"* I too have heard more times than I would like to compute that *"hurt people, hurt people"*. If I were a betting person, I would challenge this perception with thought provoking questions, such as: is it only *"hurt people that hurt people"*; do all *"hurt people, hurt people"*? This phrase in itself is thought provoking.

In her book, *Hurt(ING) People Hurt People, But God Heals ALL Wounds: Short Stories with Long Lasting Effects, author Neet Frazier-Diggs* challenges her readers with an hypothesis [*"but what if"*]. When hurting, it is often hard to look forward to the *"but, what if"*. I am reminded of a time in my life that hurt seemed to be my first and last name. I got out of bed in the morning hurting and returned after retiring for evening the same way, hurting. Hurting mentally, emotional, spiritually and physically. How can one entertain a *"but, what if"* under these types of circumstances.

There is a favorite passage of Scripture that gave me hope in those dark moments. This is an often quoted and a commonly missed quoted Scripture; *"all things work together for good"*. When the Apostle Paul was encouraging God's people in Rome, he understood that they were under the hand of a task master. They were tired and hurting. The Apostle starts the chapter in Romans eight by saying, *"there is therefore now no condemnation to those who are in Christ Jesus…"*[verse 1a] and throughout the chapter, he is committed to encouraging hurting people. By the time he gets to verse eight-teen, he wants the people to know that this hurt [*suffering*] cannot be compared to the glory [*wonder, splendor, beauty*] that shall be revealed.

By the time he makes his way to verse twenty-eight, he is able to say with great confidence, "***And we know*** *that all things work together for good to those who love God and are called according to His purpose*" (Romans 8:28).

So, what does this mean to the hurting people that are not able to grasp this concept? What happens to those that would dare say, "*this does not apply to me*". Author Neet Frazier-Diggs provides a contrast to consider, "*but, what if*", "*Hurt People Hurt People, BUT God can heal all your wounds*". This would challenge the "*hurting people*" to have the audacity [bold risk] to consider that she may be on to something.

Hurt(ING) People Hurt People, But God Heals ALL Wounds Short stories with Long Lasting Effects is the book for you if you are willing to consider a new perspective on the phrase, "*hurting people, hurt people*". The Scripture in Revelation encourages us with these life-giving words, "*and they overcame him by the blood of the Lamb, and by the word of their testimony*"; (Rev. 12:11 in part). May the testimonies of Author Neet help to change your perception of the phrase, "*hurt people, hurt people*" and provide hope in the midst of darkness that will provide the needed light for your way forward.

Your Friend,

Pastor Alethia Lance

Introduction

For every problem, there is a solution. We always hear the saying: "Hurt people hurt people" and as we look from the natural eyes that statement may be very true. The problem is that some of us accept it as not only THE truth, but as OUR truth and use it for our story and we allow it to be a part of who we become. The things that hurt us become the part of our lives that we just can't seem to let go of and sometimes even the part that we hold on to the tightest.

Hurt people hurt people has become a term that we hear and are ok with saying "that's just the way it is" or throw around loosely, but give no thought to what it really means. It has become a cliché, we consistently repeat to give an excuse for behaviors we can't explain about people we really don't know or even care to get to know.

The solution is this: the Bible says *"that death and life are in the power of the tongue"* (Proverbs 18:21), what you continue to say will at some point manifest itself. Although I've only been on this earth a short time, I have come to realize that we sometimes get conditioned to the many things that are happening in life and because we don't know how to handle them, we just accept them, instead of challenging them. We get into a habit of allowing things to get into our spirit and then conveniently use them as excuses without even thinking about the words that we are saying. We begin to allow them to fester and then when God speaks to us to challenge our habits and behaviors, we want to fight against God, however, that's not the time to resist, that is not the time to fight, it is the time to listen and obey.

A time to be still and come to know who God is and who He created us to be. God knew that the only way that we could get through life and what it had to offer (good, bad or indifferent), was to stay in constant relationship with Him. For this reason, even after the first Adam sinned, He allowed His Son, the 2nd Adam, to not only come to earth and live out every example of Love possible, but to also experience every form of hurt possible.

Therefore, being fully man, Christ was wrapped in the flesh and the Father breathed the manual that would give us the answer to everything that the enemy would try to use to hinder or prevent us on this journey to return back to Him. One of the awesome things (one amongst so many others) about God is that He teaches us to always trust Him and His plan no matter what life may bring our way. 2 Corinthians 5:17 states: *"Therefore, if any man be in Christ, he is a new creature: old things are passed away; behold, all things have become new."*

This scripture, often quoted by many, but not always put into practice, is one that many believers (including myself) have often said, but don't take literally. The truth is the reason that people continue to hurt others is because somewhere down on the inside, they are still hurting. If a person is no longer hurting, they will have no feeling of wanting to hurt someone else. So, in reality, it's not just that hurt people hurt people, but the truth is that the reason we continue to hurt others is because there's a part of us where we have not allowed old things to pass away and all things to become new and something on the inside is still hurting.

In order to become new, we must renew ourselves daily, we must close the door on the old things and open the door for new things to come in. The reason that Jesus was able to say "Father forgive them" was because He didn't hold anything in his heart against those that had hurt Him. *He was no longer hurting about what they had done, although He was hurting for them because He knew that they didn't know what they were really doing*.

He knew His purpose. He knew that His fight was not *against flesh and blood, but against principalities, against powers, against the rulers of the darkness of this world, and against spiritual wickedness in high places*. (Ephesians 6:12) He knew that what they didn't know was that He would rise again. It is now our job to seek a relationship with God so that His power can rise up within us.

We should want nothing to hold us back from doing what He has placed us on earth to do. We must know that even before we were a seed planted in our mother's womb, our omniscient "all knowing" God knew that there would be many parts of life that would hurt. Therefore knowing that hurt was inevitable and knowing that being renewed was a part of life, yet knowing that we would need to be restored in order for hurt not to continue hurting others. He then put an infallible plan into place.

God knew that in this life there would be situations that would take place due to our sinful nature and would cause us to react because that is the way that sin handles sin. In 1 Thessalonians 5:17, He told us to *"Pray without ceasing",* when we pray and seek God and give our hurts over to Him, He heals the hurt, when He heals the hurt, we are no longer hurting in the area that we have allowed Him to heal. However, we could have one area healed and another area that still needs healing, so we must continue to pray and allow God to do spiritual surgery to heal all the wounds that cause us pain and try to hinder us from growing on this journey called "Life".

Just maybe, but what if?

One day I heard someone make the statement "hurt people hurt people", as I had heard many times before and have even said it a few times myself. This time, I also heard God whisper, "but God can heal all your wounds". Believe it or not, my first thoughts were... really God? I began to think about all the people in the world hurting and thought in my mind: there's going to be a lot more hurting, a lot more wounds, and we have no control over people and their actions. As if I was telling God what was going on with the people in the world and what He could do with the creatures whom He created. (you know sometimes we try to do that) I said to Him, "we have no control over how people act and what has happened to them to make them act the way they do".

Although, in my head, what I was saying made sense to me, the Whisperer just continued to whisper. As I listened to the still small voice. I began to think, hmmm...what if this is really true? What if there was an alternate plan and every negative could be made positive? Remember in school when the teacher said "two negatives make a positive"? At the time, you sit in class wondering how double negatives could make a positive. Well this is where we finally get to see how negatives and positives work for real (and you thought you were never going to use it again). Now the Whisperer kept whispering and I kept listening, by this time He really had my attention, but I still had some doubt. Here comes the "What If", but what if we focused more on the latter than the former? *"God can heal all your wounds."* I know I'm not telling you anything new but just amuse me for a brief moment. "*What if*" the wounds are just scars that remind us that we made it through the battle? "*What if*" when we looked at the wounds, we remembered the pain and didn't want anyone else to feel what we felt?

What if we put this philosophy into place and realized that because we have been hurt, we don't have to continue the cycle. If we don't want to continue the cycle because it's painful; we would therefore work to break the cycle. It's true, we may not be able to save the world, but we can save somebody or somebodies, one body at a time. In realizing that if a cycle can be broken, which we know that it can be, we can then change our thought process and intentionally work hard to produce good fruit when we have been hurt in order not to continue to hurt and then hurt others.

This process of breaking the cycle would cause one less hurting person to not hurt the next person that would then in turn not hurt the next person. That would then not hurt the next person and then not hurt the next person and so on and so on, well you get it! Sounds simple, right? In my head that was a WOW God moment but once again I began to question: "God are you really saying that you are able to put my broken pieces back together again"? Are you saying that there is a way for me to have experienced hurt but not to continue hurting so that it doesn't hurt me the way that it was planned?

So yes, the conversation with God continued. God you mean everything that I went through was designed to grow me and not to hinder me or stop me? Are you saying that what I've gone through could make me better and not bitter? The Greek philosopher Epictetus said,

"It's not what happens to you, but how you react to it that matters". Charles Swindoll said, "I am convinced that life is 10% what happens to me and 90% how I react to it". And so it is with you...we are in charge of our attitudes."

God says it this way, *"But as for you, ye thought evil against me; but God meant it unto good..." Genesis 50:20.* You see, it is true, we cannot change what has happened to us in the past and we CANNOT change what people think about us, what they say, or even what they do. What we can do is take control of our own actions and determine what we will do with what they did or are doing to harm us. God will not allow it to take us out, but He will use it for our good if we allow Him the opportunity. He will use it to make us better and use it as a stepping stone. As God told David, *I will make thine enemies thy footstool* (Psalm 110:1) and He will do the same for us.

You see as God ministered to me and I saw the possibility of a different me there also came another possibility. Maybe I'm not the only one that feels this way and if this is ministering to me maybe it could minister to someone else. Then came the spirit of guilt, shame and disappointment. Why would anyone listen to me, who would want to hear me? What could I tell somebody else as messed up as I am? So God, being the awesome God that He is, reminded me of Amos and David. Amos, was 'just' a shepherd and a fruit picker with no education and no priestly background when God called him and used him to become the prophet to bring messages to the people of Israel about their sin. I'm sure we all have probably heard about David. David was 'just' a shepherd boy in the field tending the sheep when he was anointed by Samuel to be king over Judah.

So then I thought if this can just help one hurting person, not to hurt another person then I've done what God has told me to do. Yes it is true that hurt people hurt people, but that is because most of the time, they are still hurting in some manner. Hurting people continue to hurt people and as long as they are hurting, they will keep hurting them over and over again. Therefore, I'm 'just a' messenger sharing with you what God ministered to me that has changed my life forever. As you read this book, I pray that *'just maybe'* the words will minister to you as they did to me. **But *'what if'*** it also changes your life forever as it did for me. My prayer as you read this, if you are hurting that you will begin to search the scriptures and allow our Almighty God to heal your wounds. *He is able to do exceeding abundantly above all that you ask or think, according to the power that worketh in you* (Ephesians 3:20).

Just my perspective…

You see in my life I thought I had gone through what I had considered some very difficult times. *From my perspective* all of my wounds were open, all of my wounds were exposed, and all of my wounds grew with me and as I became an adult. They were being hit over and over again. I felt like I was just bleeding out and God wasn't doing anything about it. However, I couldn't see it then, but things in my life were probably no worse than many and possibly a whole lot better than others. Sometimes we just don't see clearly when we're twirling in the midst of the storm. We create an image of what life is supposed to be or we allow people to tell us what life is supposed to be and then we put pressure on ourselves to live up to those expectations. We also allow people to tell us who we're supposed to be and what we're supposed to do to be successful in life (whatever successful means). I'm not sure if we ever even figure it out because as you grow up and become mature, you realize that success means different things to different people. What may be success for one may not be as important to another.

I've also learned that success is not so much about where you are but how far you have come. I've learned that as we go through life we work and we try to do all the things that we imagined or thought would make us successful. You go to school, you get the degrees, you marry the love of your life, you have a family with 2.5 children and live in a nice house with the white picket fence in a nice neighborhood. You're driving a nice car and after you think you have finally reached success, one day you wake up and realize that what you thought was success is not really success at all. You realize that everything you based success on and worked hard to accomplish could be taken away in a matter of a moment. In a moment your life can change and everything you had achieved was temporary, if it wasn't built on a solid foundation.

Those same friends that put you on a pedestal will not even speak to you; and you may even feel empty and broken. When everything you thought made you who you were is gone, you realize that what you thought was living, was not really life at all. You are mad, you are angry and you are now one hurting individual. At this critical point of reality, instead of falling on your knees with the little bit of breath and dignity that you have left, you walk around for years trying to survive and pretend that everything is okay, but hating God and blaming everything on Him.

It seems like everyone around you is just watching you. You are bleeding out and no one will even give you a band aid to cover your wound. You tell yourself that these are the very same people that say, "I'm your friend, I'll be there for you, you can call on me anytime" but yet when they see the blood dripping, they won't answer your call because they've heard your story over and over again. Once again, you realize, you can't blame them, these people are doing the same thing in life that you are doing. They are trying to survive, they are trying to figure out life for themselves and they are trying to find their purpose and do what they believe they were put here to do. You don't see their blood, you don't see their pain, you only see yourself and what you need because while you're twirling in the storm, your vision is blurred.

Yes, their story may be different than yours and they may have it together a little bit better than you because they have been practicing a little longer. They may be dealing with their tragedies, insecurities and hurts differently than you are. They may have learned how to deal with their pain a bit differently than you have but they are still dealing with it. Better yet, while you think they have it all together, what you don't know is that they are crying out to God in the midnight hours while you are thinking you can fix it all by yourself. The difference is they have learned to trust God and take Him at His Word. They don't have the answers for your life just as you don't have the answers for theirs. Now don't get me wrong, I'm not saying that God doesn't give us people to help us throughout this journey, because He does. After all, it's all a part of Him teaching us to serve one another and to grow together. As a matter of fact, He designed it so that you can't do it alone. He designed it so that you need someone and you long for someone to help you through it.

Remember in the beginning, *Genesis 2:18, "**And the Lord God said, it is not good that man should be alone**"*. So yes, it was from the very beginning that God had a plan for no one to be alone or do it alone, but to need others along the way; but when life happens, you spend years separating yourself and trying to do it all by yourself. You think the answer is, if you don't depend on anyone else, you won't get disappointed or hurt again, right? Wrong answer! It's impossible to do it alone because we were not created to do it alone.

You see, I was still that little girl who didn't know how to handle the pain in my own life. I grew up angry, afraid and withdrawn on the inside but wearing a mask on the outside. *From my perspective*, I didn't talk about it or even try to think about it. I didn't consider myself a victim and I thought I was over it. In reality, I was living with a victim mentality because every time I went through something painful I allowed it to cause me to be down and depressed. It rendered me powerless. You may say, aren't we supposed to let it go and step back and give it to God? Yes, we are but in my case it was avoidance. If I didn't think about it and didn't deal with it, it would go away. Aaaahh wrong again!!!

It hindered my growth and prolonged my healing and kept me hurting. I was hurting and instead of allowing God to heal my wounds, I was hurting others. My actions, behaviors, and decisions hurt others but most of all I hurt God because I wasn't living the life that He had sent me here to live. Yes, I was a Christian but I wasn't living life to the fullest. I was merely existing and surviving to get through life. I was doing what people expected me to do on the outside and maybe even what I was expecting myself to do but I was miserable. I was suffering in silence and

I was dying. I was literally committing suicide and I didn't even care. I wanted to get out of this place of hurting anyway I could.

I wanted to leave the world and the people who had hurt me so badly because I didn't know how to add the negatives to make them positive. Yes, I knew what the Bible said and I read it and studied it because of course that was another thing I was told and expected to do. But in my reading and studying, I was still so bitter. Yes, I went to church and I praised God because I knew that He had gotten me out of some pretty bad situations. I knew that if He hadn't brought me out, life would have been so much worse than it was.

Yet I was still angry and bitter. I grew up in church all my life, I saw people from many different churches praise God and then it seemed like God just wasn't very good to them. It seemed like they struggled to get ahead but they never got anywhere, at least from what I could see. It seemed like they were always going through but never getting out. They constantly praised God and when life happened I saw them laying on the altar for days crying just to get through again. Of course, God would answer their prayer to help them to hold on a little while longer. Before you knew it something else was taking place and there they were laying on the altar crying out to God again. On the flip side, these same people had secrets to be kept and testimonies that were never told. It was because of the saying: "what goes on in this house stays in this house" and sometimes that was even the house of God.

What I didn't realize was that while I was so busy mentally judging I was missing the power of God. It was those same prayers and their laying on the altar and crying out to God that was keeping them emotionally stable and keeping them from literally losing their mind. It was their crying out to God that was keeping them from physically hurting someone and making a bad situation worse. It was their crying out to God that saved them from doing something that they would have lived to regret for the rest of their lives because they made one poor decision during a temporary moment of insanity.

Now I knew that God was good, as a matter a fact, I knew that He was great, but when life happened, I didn't think I could trust Him with everything because He didn't always seem to make things work out like I thought they would and I definitely didn't think He was working anything out for my good. *From my perspective*, in my little finite mind, people were always suffering and they never seemed to get anywhere. In my mind, Jesus came to earth, suffered, bled and then died for a bunch of people who didn't even care to love Him.

It appeared that He went through all of this for nothing, but boy was I wrong! When I looked from the outside I just saw people going through trauma just to learn a lesson and that wasn't something I could comprehend. To me it was better to just check out while you were ahead and skip all the nonsense and what I considered the games of life. Why did people want to live anyway? The world was crazy and people were cruel and doesn't the Bible say in 2 Corinthians 5:8, ***to be absent from the body is to be present with the Lord***? I never understood why people were so happy to wake up every morning.

It appeared that God had a plan and a way of doing life that appeared to be a vicious cycle. It looked like we would never win although the Bible says we do in the end and if you read to the end of the story, we win really "Big"! Now once I really grew up and began to experience life for myself, I realized that I had it all wrong and I realized that I was missing the Bigger picture. I learned that in God's infinite wisdom, He wants us to grow and draw closer to Him. Life may offer us some challenges but everything we go through in life is for a reason. Even when it seems hard, if we trust Him, spend time with Him and get to know Him for who He really is (and also get to know ourselves for who He created us to be); we will then see that the negative will **never** outweigh the positive. Although life may not always make sense, it will work out in our favor.

What is This…

This book is a mix of stories with people facing real life situations. It's about how we try to live life on our own and concern ourselves more about image and religion rather than God and relationship. It's about not just seeing the problem, but looking into another perspective to see the solution. Not just seeing the glass as half empty or even as half full, but even in the midst of a twirling storm, knowing that life can challenge you and the glass can go from half empty to half full really quick or vice versa, depending on your perspective.

Yes, the problem is always going to present itself, but the solution is always available if you seek God and just look a little closer. If you trust God and allow Him to instruct you through His Word in the midst of it all and follow His word, your cup will become full and running over.

Will it stay full…well that's up to you…everyday is a part of your journey and every day, you must make the decision to choose life.

The chapter titles in this book may seem a bit contradictory, as there are two sides to every coin. There is the part of one's life that we see and a part that is hidden to most. The only way that the hidden part is able to be healed is if we are willing to apply God's Word to the hurting part and allow Him to heal our wounds. The stories in this book are told from two perspectives. The outward part that is seen, **(the problem)** which is actually the result of the inward part or the root that is hidden. Then there is **the solution** or the Word of God that is needed to stop the hurting and to heal the wound. Maybe it's your story or maybe it's not. Maybe you just know somebody who went through it. Whatever the case, I'm sure many of us will be able to relate either directly or indirectly.

The question is will you allow it to make you bitter or will it make you better? Life is a choice, God wants us to choose life, but He will not force us to choose anything! Read this book with an open heart and an open mind. If any of this applies to you, know that God is preparing a table before you to allow your cup to run over. He wants to heal you where you're hurting so that his blood, not yours, will drip on others. Even when everything around you is saying you can't, know that with God all things are possible and He is saying, *"My child, my grace is sufficient for thee: for my strength is made perfect in weakness" (2 Corinthians 12:9)*, you can trust Him.

Chapter 1 – Ian's Story

Rape by Consent: Dealing with Low Self-Esteem

Looking from the Outside

Ian's life was full of trauma. As a young boy he experienced so

many feelings of insecurity. Sometimes to get away from it all he would

just hide and no one could find him. Growing up, he always felt like he

was doing something wrong and it seemed like the harder he tried, the

more he was knocked down. He felt like he was treated as if he could

never do anything right. Due to the damage to his self-esteem, he lost his

voice and would never speak up for himself because he was afraid that he

would say the wrong thing. As he became older, he was still very passive

and would keep his feelings hidden. He never wanted to confront anyone

but instead he would just try to please everyone.

Even when he didn't want to do something, he couldn't say no.

Since Ian didn't know how to deal with his feelings and was afraid of

disappointing others, he would get frustrated and tired of everyone. He

would do what he did as a child and hide. He just couldn't seem to find

the boldness to speak up and say how he was really feeling. He didn't

have many friends and he lived by himself so now when he was hiding nobody was looking for him during his lowest moments. He wouldn't go to work and he wouldn't respond to calls from the job. He would just hide like a turtle in a shell. Of course, he had several different jobs because every time he had a good one, he would lose it due to poor attendance.

Ian had many talents but he was always too insecure to step out and take the lead. Many things that may have been difficult to others seemed to come naturally to him. Whenever he did work on a project he would always volunteer to be behind the scenes. He never wanted any eyes on him. Not only would he not speak up for himself, he could never be true to who he really was. Sometimes, it just seemed easier to not try than to try and have everyone see him as a failure. He allowed the enemy to deceive him and say: "Do you really think you are good enough for that?" He allowed the enemy to speak to him and he always listened to his lies.

All the time he knew that in these moments that satan was deceiving him but he would give in to the temptation. He was comfortable in this familiar place. He was full of anxiety about life but on the inside, he knew that there was more that he was supposed to do. He just didn't know how he was going to have the guts to do it yet he was unsatisfied and disappointed with his life. He was miserable knowing that he was not doing what he was put on earth to do. But "what if I fail", he thought. "What if you try and it really works out?," another voice said. "What if I fail God and can't do what I'm really supposed to do in this life" or "what if I finally do and then get to the top and fall back down again?"

These feelings of low self-esteem, inadequacy and insecurity constantly nagged Ian. Every now and then, he would peek out and use his gifts and it felt so good as if it was natural. But that only lasted a moment. Before you knew it, that little insecure head would peek back out and once again he was feeling like a nobody. He convinced himself that he couldn't do anything right. Unfortunately, Ian couldn't see the gifts and talents that God had given him. He was blinded by despair and even when someone told him how gifted he was, he didn't know how to accept the compliment. He still felt that he wasn't doing anything special. He felt like the things he did could be done by anyone. He heard what people said but he just always felt like he wasn't good enough. He would beat himself up and he would always tell himself that he needed to try harder but he felt that he just couldn't.

Ian's Prayer:

Dear God,

The feeling of fear and anxiety is overwhelming and unbearable. I know you created me in your image, so why do I not feel good about myself when I know that your love is more than enough? Why do I not hold my head up but instead I allow these feelings to overtake me? Why do I hold on to the shame of the things that have happened to me and blame and devalue myself? Why do I feel like there's more but I'm hurting so bad and I'm afraid to try? I don't want to open myself up to being hurt over and over again. You have taught me to love others but I isolate myself because it is so hard for me to love myself. I continue to forgive others but it's hard for me to forgive myself. Help me God to look to you as my creator, I know I am not perfect, but you designed me perfectly. You have put everything in me that I need to fulfill my purpose in this life. Help me to see myself as you see me. Show me the mirror that you see me through. Give me insight so that I may hold my head up and not down. I love you for creating me and I need your help. Help me to accept myself and feel the love that you felt when you were creating me.

Signed,

Insecure Ian

The Problem ~ One Perspective

The Bible says in John 10:10, "The thief cometh not, but for to steal and to kill, and to destroy; I am come that they might have life, and they might have it more abundantly." The enemy comes to steal your joy and most of all steal your peace. He totally sucks the life out of you and every day you are depleted. You have no strength to deal with anything. Most days you do just enough to get by. You allow the enemy to keep you bound. I call this process allowing the enemy to rape you with your consent. You say wow rape is such a strong word to use, that's a bit insensitive when so many are raped and scarred for the rest of their lives. Rape is a very strong word and it is exactly why it's being used.

What does it mean to be raped? It means that someone has violently abused you and taken away your rights. It means that they have taken something from you without your permission and have taken your goods or property to leave you with a void or empty feeling. In a rape case, the victim may choose to tell or not to tell for whatever reason they feel is right for them. There could be feelings of shame, guilt or maybe even the feeling that they caused it or brought it on themselves. No matter what the reason, one thing every victim would agree to is that they didn't want it to happen or they didn't ask for it. Why would anyone allow the enemy to do this or consent to his actions?

If it is something that is despised and looked upon as cruel, vulgar or so distasteful, why does the enemy have permission to keep one in bondage? Why would one allow the enemy to abuse them on a daily basis? Every time he comes, you listen. Every time he comes, you entertain him. Every time a trial comes, you get down and depressed. You say you're sick of him and you don't want to be bothered but yet you allow him to come into your house and take your goods.

The Solution ~ Another Perspective

Abundant life: this is what Christ died for and has promised to us all. From the time that one is born Jesus wants you to walk into your created purpose and have abundant life. This is the plan that is created by the Father. *Jeremiah 1:5* **says, "*Before I formed thee in the belly I knew thee; and before thou camest forth out of the womb I sanctified thee, and I ordained thee a prophet unto the nations".* (KJV)**

God has given each of us gifts and talents. He has given us everything that we need to get the job done that he has placed us here to complete. So even before conception, God had a plan. The enemy will do anything to try to prevent God's plan for you to come to fruition. Although he may not know the full plan, he knows that if God has created you and has allowed you to come into the Earth, that God has a purpose. In knowing that God has a plan, satan begins to develop his plan, to prevent the purpose from being fulfilled. From the time a baby is born, a mother can encounter many risks or face various challenges during pregnancy.

This can include anything from pre-existing health conditions, age, thoughts of abortion, miscarriages, etc. The process of pregnancy is not easy and should not be taken lightly. Carrying the newborn can become very stressful and is different for every woman, but nothing can stop God's plan. *"For I know the thoughts that I think toward you, saith the Lord, thoughts of peace , and not of evil, to give you an expected end." (Jeremiah 29:11)*

"God created man in his own *image, in the image of God created him; male and female created him." Genesis 1:27.* There's a reason God gave the command to train up a child, *Proverbs 22:6 "Train*

up a child in the way he should go: and when he is old, he will not depart from it." Training begins at day one or even in the womb, as it is told. As a baby grows to become a child, they live life innocently. One has no cares about the world. Jesus says in *Matthew 6:25, "Therefore I say unto you, "Take no thought for your life, what ye shall eat, or what ye shall drink; nor yet for your body, what ye shall put on. Isn't life more than meat, and the body more than raiment?"*

That's how life is supposed to be lived, by taking no thought. That's not to say that you don't make plans, but the plan is to seek the Creator for the life that He has planned for you. You want to know why God wants us to be like little children? During the infant stage, one is actually doing what God created them to do by living life with no thought of what is to come. God gives a child a parent so that they may be protected and shielded, guarded from the world and the painful journey that will come just from being in this world. Parents are not perfect and sometimes, unfortunately, the very ones that are supposed to protect you and take care of you for life, may be the very ones to destroy your life.

Even with this, Jesus knew these dangers would come, nothing takes Him by surprise. In John 16:33, Jesus said, *"These things I have spoken unto you, that in me ye might have peace. In the world ye shall have tribulation: but be of good cheer; I have overcome the world."*

Yes life has a way of happening to us all. Whether you are born with a silver spoon or a plastic spoon in your mouth, life will happen. No matter how hard a parent may try, life will happen. No matter how much you are protected, life will happen. Why? Because life is a growing experience. It is the vehicle in which God has given for one to live, love and laugh. But it is also the vehicle in which He has given to learn, serve, and grow. No one is exempt, everyone has their ups and downs.

The question is: what will you do when life's challenges try to get the best of you? Will you hand over your goods to the enemy and let him take you hostage; and allow your gifts and talents to be hidden because you back down and live in the shadows? Will you stay in a place of hurting and use your words to hurt and abuse others because you choose not to deal with the fact that you let the enemy take your stuff? Or will you trust God and allow the pain that you have endured make you stronger and use your testimony to help someone else?

Hurting People Hurt People, But God HEALS ALL Wounds…

Ian was hurt by someone who was still hurting. Although he would cry out to God for help, he was so wounded that he wasn't allowing his wounds to be healed by the healer. Ian grew up with low self-esteem. It caused him to be withdrawn. It caused him to hide and hide his gifts. It caused him to allow satan to steal from him what God had freely given to him. Ian had to make a choice. God wants us to make a choice.

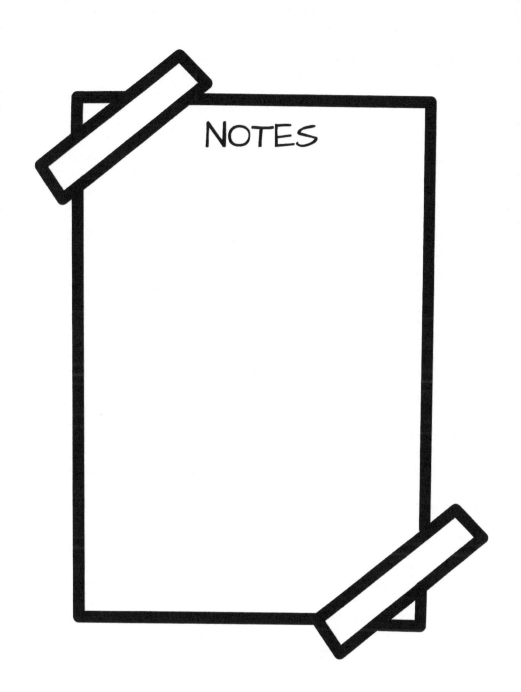

NOTES

Chapter 2 – Thomas' Story

The Secret That Was Never Told But Worn:

Dealing with Domestic Violence

Looking from the Outside

Thomas, why is your life like this? Why do you still hold on to

the very secret that will destroy you? Why are you always angry, why do

you beat your wife and then say you're sorry? Why? It's because

Thomas was hurting and instead of getting help, he held it all in. He

never told anyone that growing up as a young man, he watched his father

beat his mother consistently. Then at age ten, his older brother shot his

father's best friend because he caught him in the bed with his mother. He

could never tell anyone because he had to take the fall for his older

brother because he would have been charged as a minor, while his older

brother would have been charged as an adult. As a minor he only had to

serve 15 years and would still have a life once he was released. So

instead of telling what he thought that no one would ever believe, he kept

it all inside.

He kept all his pain tucked away in a place that he thought was

hidden. Thomas never thought that he would be this way but to hear him say it, he didn't know what happened to him. But he was always angry. He was angry but he didn't know how to express the anger that was on the inside so he expressed it in unhealthy ways. He would drink just so he didn't have to feel the pain and then he would get so drunk that he didn't remember what happened. He never remembered coming home smelling like alcohol and his wife having to undress him and put him to bed. Most of the time he never even remembered how he got home. When he would wake up the next morning, still drunk from the night before, he would find a reason to argue and fight. The fight was never really a fight but instead just a beating for his wife. Beatings that would produce bruises that would cause her to stand in the mirror with tears rolling down her face, covering her bruises with makeup and making excuses to herself for what happened. He said he didn't mean it, he said he would never do it again. He also said he didn't know how to express his anger but he did. He did it in a way that caused the one woman that he said he loved, much pain. He expressed it in a way that made other people hurt. But why?

Thomas had spent 15 years in jail. Doing time for a crime that he didn't commit. When he was finally released, he met a very beautiful woman who treated him like a king. They fell in love and married quickly but what she didn't know was that there was a side of Thomas that she had never seen. He never told his new wife about his past life and she never asked. He was fine until it was very difficult for him to find a job and he couldn't take care of his family. The pressures of life started to build and that's when he started to drink. He was told that a man only cries if he's weak so every time he wanted to cry, he bottled up all those tears. He would get drunk, go home and beat the woman that always took care of him.

The woman that wanted him to know that she loved him in spite of his deepest and darkest secrets. The one woman who would tell him that he was more than a conqueror but what she didn't know was that he was still the little boy who went to prison. She would tell him that he could be anything he wanted to be and that she loved him and appreciated him for keeping their family together. She was the one that he would beat every time he had the opportunity. Not because he didn't love her but because he didn't know how to express that he loved her in a loving way. So why did he beat her? Why did he come home more nights than he could even care to remember and beat her when she was only trying to love him? He beat her because his father beat his mother and he went to prison for his brother. These were the people that said they loved him.

He didn't really know what love was. He couldn't recognize that this woman loved him and she treated him in a way that wasn't familiar. Instead of loving her back, he beat her. He held the guilt and shame of watching his mother get beat all those years and not doing anything about it, so that's why he took the fall. He thought taking the fall would change the guilt. He thought taking the fall would mean he stood up in some way, but it didn't. It had him locked up with shame and even after he had been physically released, he didn't know how to get out of the prison in his mind that had tormented him for so long. He didn't know how to forgive his father for beating his mother. He didn't know how to forgive his brother for killing and letting him take the blame. He didn't know how to forgive the prison guards who abused him. He wore the pain every day and because he wore the pain, he became the pain inflictor. ...

Thomas' Prayer:

Ok God,

Since you have allowed all of this to happen to me, tell me what I'm supposed to do now. Tell me how to deal with all this anger that I didn't even know was there. The wonderful woman that you gave me is not going to stick around much longer when I can't take care of her and allow me to keep using her as a punching bag. She's not going to put up with my behaviors and abuse. I can't blame her. I know I can't keep treating her this way but God why won't you help me. I constantly take my anger out on her because I can't stand up and take it out on the people who really hurt me. I'm hurting God, don't you feel my pain? I can't stand up to my family and tell them how they made me feel. I don't want to lose her God, but I know I don't deserve her and she doesn't deserve this pain I'm putting her through. Please give me the strength to stop this pain once and for all. I cry out to you because you know me on the inside, even the parts that I won't share with anyone, you know. I need your help. I can't do this on my own.

Signed,

Tormented Thomas

The Problem ~ One Perspective

How can one describe a broken heart? According to Webster's, anything that is broken is violently separated into parts or shattered. A broken heart is often used to represent a physical and indescribable feeling in which an individual may be experiencing a deep hurt for one reason or another. In Psalm 147, the writer describes a people that are broken in heart, or wounded by inward pain, not only by the pain that they have caused God, but by the pain that they have caused themselves through their acts of sin. Nevertheless, God has promised that even when one is not making the best decisions or living up to their fullest potential, He yet shows mercy. However, there are times that although God shows mercy, one does not know how to extend mercy to themselves. In that case, it is hard to let go and hard to move on.

It is said that church hurt is the worst kind of hurt and why is that? Is it because it comes from someone that you think wouldn't hurt you? Is it because we believe that Christians are not supposed to hurt us? What makes it so painful? Is it because it was my church friend, the one whom I sat with and shared memories? It made it hard for me to accept.

But the truth is we often expect so much more from our brothers and sisters than we do from others. We sometimes forget that they may be broken too. We are to be our brother's and sister's keeper so we must understand that none of us are perfect and sometimes even when we don't mean to, we have the ability to hurt or let others down. The difference is the way that we are supposed to be able to handle it. Can I go to my brother and ask for forgiveness or do I just hold it all in and allow the pain to fester?

The Solution ~ Another Perspective

"Forgiveness"

In Matthew 18:21 Peter asked a question: ***"Lord, how many times do I forgive a person if they continue to hurt me, is it enough to forgive them seven times? Jesus responded with an answer I'm sure Peter wasn't expecting. He said not just seven times, but seventy times seven"***. In other words, God does not expect us to track how many times we must forgive a person, but rather do it as unto the Lord. Each day, no matter how hard we try to get it right, there is something that we do that God must forgive us for. Therefore, as He forgives us, He also wants us to forgive others. Forgiveness does not mean that you let people walk all over you, nor does it mean that you let them off the hook for the wrong that they have done.

Instead it means that you don't hold it over their head, nor expect them to continue to repay you for the wrong over and over again. Forgiveness also releases you from holding a grudge and being angry. Doing so, causes you to harbor hatred and strife in your heart. It relieves you of the energy of reliving the pain and allows you to redirect that energy to do the will of God and focus on the purpose that He has called for your life. Although forgiving someone that hurt you may not be easy, one way to try to release yourself from holding on is to try to walk in that person's shoes and see yourself through their eyes.

This is not to give a person an excuse for the wrong that they have done but sometimes people hurt people because they are hurting and need help themselves. Sometimes forgiving a person can open your heart to help the person that hurt you. Does that mean that there will always be reconciliation? Absolutely not! Sometimes that may not be possible and sometimes you may have to love people from a distance. However, there are times when God will use the very situation that you thought caused you the most damage to cause you the most growth. Forgiving a person takes the power and control from them and gives you peace in God.

On the other hand, unforgiveness opens the door for the enemy to constantly have control over you, bringing in bitterness, strife and anger. It opens the door for one to feel the need for revenge, when God says: *"vengeance is mine; I will repay" (Romans, 12:19)*. I'm not going to tell you that forgiving someone that has hurt you is easy because in our own power, it's not even possible. But I will tell you that with God all things are possible and we can definitely *"do all things through Christ which gives us strength," Philippians 4:13.* Yes it may take days, months and sometimes even years for you to get it right. But God does not ask us to do anything that He will not also give us the power to produce.

But as in the scripture, God assures us that He has forgiven us of the very sin that would keep one bound. In *Psalm 103: 12 God says, "as far as the east is from the west, so far as he removed our transgressions from us."* Therefore, when God forgives, He wholeheartedly forgives and nothing can take one back to that sinful state, except for oneself. According to *Proverbs 26:11, "as a dog returneth to his vomit, so a fool returneth to his folly".* After you are forgiven, God wants you to make a change, not return to foolishness and not continue to beat up on yourself or beat up on anyone else for the wrong that was done. Once a person can look past the past, they are able to pick themselves up and make a change.

God promises to bind up the bleeding wounds and cause one to rejoice. He said in Psalm 40:2-3: *"He brought me up also out of a horrible pit, out of the miry clay, and set my feet upon a rock,* **and** *established my goings. And he hath put a new song in my mouth,* **even** *praise unto our God: many shall see* it, *and fear, and shall trust in the LORD".* If God is able to forgive and then do all of that, why would one hold on to such pain on their own? God promises in *Isaiah 61:3 that "He would give you beauty for ashes, the oil of joy for mourning, the garment of praise for the spirit of heaviness".* God desires one to have so much joy and so much peace that He makes promises for life to be so much more than one could ever imagine.

Hurting People Hurt People, But God HEALS ALL Wounds…

Thomas was still hurting. He held on to his pain and then caused pain to others. He didn't know how to take the word of God and apply it to his life. Although he was a young boy when many things happened that he couldn't control, he still blamed himself and even as an adult refused to accept God's forgiveness for the sins that he had committed in the past. He was hurting when he blamed himself and held himself responsible for not being able to help his mother out of a bad situation. Instead of walking in peace and victory, he walked in guilt and shame. Instead of having a peaceful life, he had a life full of misery because he was still hurting.

Jesus said in *Psalm 55:22, "Cast your burden on the Lord, and He shall sustain you."* What if Thomas was able to give his hurts and his pain over to the Lord? God is the only one that can handle the pain and burden. He knew it would be too much to carry and that's why He chose to carry it. He said in *Isaiah 41:13, "For I, the Lord your God, will hold your right hand, Saying to you, "Fear not, I will help you."* God wants us to accept all of His promises and live the victorious life of freedom. Thomas' home would have been one of peace rather than one of chaos. He could have lived a victorious life with a woman who had loved him like no other, but instead, he chose defeat.

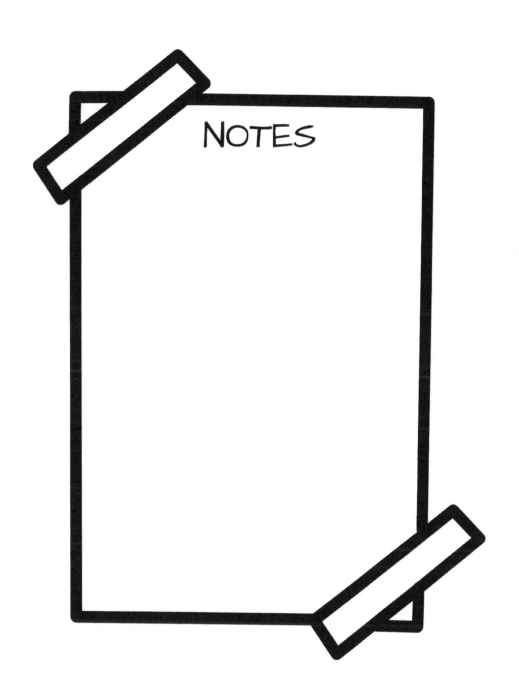

NOTES

Chapter 3 – Susan's Story

Wounded From The Womb: Dealing with Abandonment

Looking from the Outside

The love she had for him was like no other. He was her first love.

He was the one who would teach her all the things a girl should expect from a man. He was the one that she would lean on, when times were tough. The one that she would look up to. She called him "daddy" but he called her a "mistake". She was born out of lust for a woman that had his attention but would no longer give him attention.

When he couldn't have the woman, Susan was no longer a priority. The baby girl was forgotten and neglected. She grew up to long for what she would never have: a daddy that would love her like no other. She longed for a daddy that would protect her and call her his one and only. The lonely look on her face as she watched him walk out of her life seemed to last forever. In that moment, she didn't know that the pain she felt as a little girl would be there even as she grew into a full-grown woman.

Years and years went by but there was still no love from her daddy. There was just a void for the love she longed for. As she got older, she continued to long for the love of her father, hoping that one day he would acknowledge her as his little girl, his first born, the love of his life. She longed for him to tell her how beautiful she was. She longed for him to spend time with her, to take her shopping for her prom dress, or to even walk her down the aisle at her wedding. She constantly looked for him to show up, maybe at school, maybe for a show or a game or at least her high school graduation, but he never did. She never saw his face in the crowd, not once.

She finally accepted that he would never teach her how to be treated by a man so that she didn't fall for the first guy that paid her a little attention. So you guessed it…that's exactly what she did! She settled for the man who said he loved her but only used her. Susan never really knew who she was so she felt like she had no identity. She would often wonder where she developed certain features about herself. Features that she wondered if he even knew she had. Features like the color of her eyes. Did he know her favorite color; did he know what she liked to do; or what she wanted to become?

As she thought about it inwardly, she became more and more angry. No, he didn't know any of those things about her and she didn't know any of those things about him. She was often told she looked like him and she could not be denied. So why did he deny her? Why didn't he get to know her, why didn't he love her, like other daddy's loved their little girls? What would make him stay away? Finally, she convinced herself that she was better off without him. Yet all along she yearned for his love and she looked for it in every man that she ever knew. Life felt empty, there were many missing pieces, many questions, but no answers to reveal who she was.

Who was this little girl and where did she get the very things that she loved, like sports, music and traveling the world. Maybe she could ask him at one of those distant visits that they had, but nope during those visits he only wanted to know about the love that he lost so many years ago, her mother. Unfortunately, what he wanted to know couldn't be answered by Susan. Her mother left her when she was twelve and she was raised by her grandmother.

She knew her mother loved her and she would often see her at various family events. Her mother would do what she could for her when she could. In spite of all of her feelings, she continued to have hope that her daddy would make her dreams come true. One day maybe all her questions would be answered but instead she faced the one day she never dreamed of or prepared for. It was the day that she would see him lying there with no life at all. The day she got that call was worse than the day that she watched him walk out of her life because this time there was no hope for things to get better. There was no hope for him to look into her eyes and finally realize all that he had been missing. No, this time he was gone forever.

Susan's Prayer:

God,

Today I feel so empty. How could you allow me to come into this world feeling like a mistake? Why was I even born if no one really wanted me? Was I only created to suffer and feel pain? If I'm a mistake to my parents, how is anyone else going to want me? I know you said you would never leave me but I am alone and feeling lonely. I'm lost and confused. I have no guidance. No one to teach me, no one to tell me they love me and no one to tell me that I'm important to them. I'm always trying to please people but no one tries to please me. I see families together and I wonder what it would feel like to be a part of one. What will it be like to have my mother and father under one roof and for us to sit together with a real conversation or a meal together? I guess I will never know. I will never know the feeling of having my dad around to give me strength in the tough times. My Mom is living

her own life trying to fill her own voids. Will anyone really care if

I'm not here? If I run away, will anyone miss me or how long will

it even take for them to notice that I'm gone? Wow what a life to

live, what a way to grow up. Fill this void or take me away. The

pain is unbearable and I'm just a little girl. I heard that Jesus

loves little children. Does He really love me?

Signed,

Sin Born Susan

The Problem ~ One Perspective

A house that is abandoned has no one to live in it. No one cares

for it. People may go past it but they notice that there's no one taking care

of it. No one to groom the lawn, no one to sweep the porch and no one

looking out the windows. That means that they can do anything they

want to the house. Vandalize it, abuse it and even worst damage it to a

point that it will need total renovations. Web MD says that:

"Abandonment issues happen when a parent or caregiver does not

provide the child with consistent warm or attentive interactions, leaving

them feeling chronic stress and fear. The experiences that happen during a child's development will often continue into adulthood".

(Abandonment Issues, November 20, 2020)

A child suffering from abandonment may experience feelings of fear, anxiety and feel that they are always in danger. They may feel afraid and not even know why they're feeling that way. Feelings of what will happen to me? Who will take care of my essential needs? They may feel exposed or vulnerable to whatever may come their way. Sometimes one may learn things on their own but that's not the way it's supposed to be. There is supposed to be someone to look over you. Someone to make sure that you are cared for, someone to protect you and make sure that you are not abused or harmed.

As a child, being left alone can also cause many inside feelings that can never be explained. No matter what may happen in life, you may always feel like you are alone. As you grow, people may try to make you feel secure or feel that you belong but that feeling of loneliness and abandonment may never go away. Is there really a way to recover from this or do you grow up with these feelings forever and never feel like you are a part?

The Solution ~ Another Perspective

Mark 3:25 says: "*and if a house be divided against itself, that house cannot stand.*" Even if no one else believes in you, you must believe in yourself. Sometimes we can be our own worst enemy. We have to be able to release thoughts that don't serve us or do us any good. No matter what has happened in life, you must know that even when no one else is with you. God said that "*I will never leave thee nor thee*" (Hebrews 13:5). He said "*Greater is He that is in you, than He that is in world*" (1 John 4:4). Therefore, even when others forsake you, God will still be with you. If you have given your life to Him, you have the greatest on the inside of you and if you haven't given your life to Him, you must do it quickly.

You must stand on His word knowing that "*you are more than a conqueror*" (Romans 8:37), "*you are fearfully and wonderfully made.*" (Psalms 139:14) God makes no mistakes; and even if your mother and father were too young to know what they were doing, God still knew what He was doing. Romans 8:29, says: "*for whom He foreknew, He also predestined to be conformed to the image of His Son*". God knew you in the womb and knew that there was purpose and destiny inside of you and that's why He told you to come forth. Psalms 27:10 says: "*when my father and my mother forsake me. Then the LORD will take me up*". God will never abandon you. He will always be there. He knows what you need and how to make sure your needs are fulfilled. It may not come in the way you think it should or even through the people that you think it should come through but one thing for sure is that it's coming through.

Whatever He has promised, He will bring it to pass. However, in order to get through the unwanted feelings, we must give it to Him. We have to tell ourselves God's word daily so that the spirit on the inside grows stronger than the flesh on the outside. It's a daily journey! The little girl in you may feel that the worst thing that could have ever happened to you was to not have your daddy notice you. However, the spirit in you knows that the best thing that could have happened is that your Heavenly Father knows you, loves you and you are the apple of His eye. He has seen everything that you have done and knows every struggle that you have faced and is waiting to reward you with everything that a Father wants to give his child but it is up to you.

Hurting People Hurt People, But God HEALS ALL Wounds…

All through her life Susan felt alone and abandoned. Always feeling like she didn't belong made her do whatever she felt necessary to try to be a part of the crowd. Unfortunately, it also caused her to put herself in some pretty bad situations and she always stayed in trouble. She felt like if she stayed in trouble, it would at least get her some attention. But that also gave her a name of being defiant, which she really wasn't, it was just her way of acting out.

Always feeling hurt and ashamed of who she was also brought feelings of insecurity. Feelings of insecurity brought on feelings of doubt and feelings of doubt brought on feelings of depression. Therefore, because of those feelings, she would always self-sabotage her relationships and lash out at those who were the closest to her. She wanted to push them away before they had a chance to push her away. Susan wasn't just hurting those around her, she was also continuing to hurt herself.

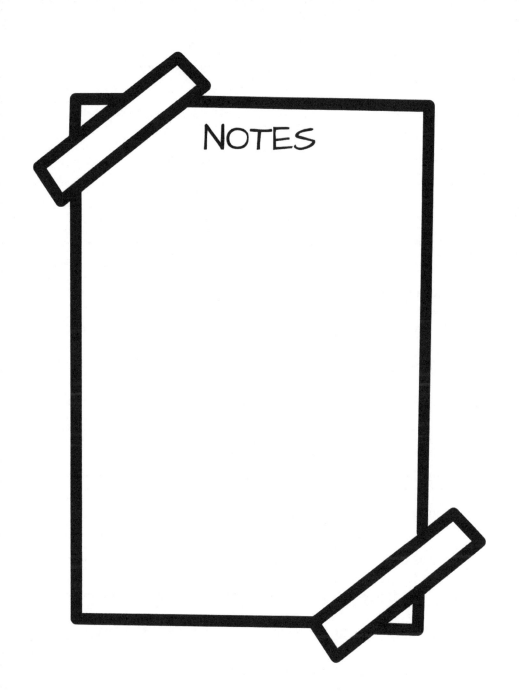

NOTES

Chapter 4 – Madeline's Story

Looking from the Outside

Madeline was molested by her father at nine years old. Every

night she lay in her bed scared to death of never knowing when he would

come into her room. She would try to stay up as late as possible because

she developed a hate for the night hours. Eventually her mother would

tell her she had been up long enough. She would plead and cry for more

time but eventually her time would be up and off to bed she had to go.

She would lay there praying and crying "Lord, please don't let him,

please don't let him come in my room tonight".

This devastating fear would continue until she fell asleep or until

she heard the door creek and it was him. Another night of torture and

another night of torment. She had to live with the trauma, the nightmares,

the fear and the pain. She cried every night not knowing what else she

could do. How can I tell anyone that this is happening? "I don't want

anyone else to be hurt so I'll just suffer alone," she said. You see, her

father had always told her that if she ever told anyone, it would break up the family and it would be all her fault. If the family were to break up, she would go to a girl's home or foster care, (she had heard this threat from her mother before, when she didn't do right). Her mother didn't work so she wouldn't be able to take care of them so they would be stuck with him. So instead of telling anyone, she just cried all the time.

She would cry when her mother left the house and she would cry when her mother came home. Her mother didn't get it. Madeline continued to pray and continued to cry with no resolve. Madeline couldn't take it anymore. The weight was too heavy on her shoulders, finally she blurted out words to her father that could not be returned, "I hate you, why do you keep doing this to me?" Her mother wondered what was going on after hearing such harsh words, so Madeline tried to tell her mother the worst story a little girl could ever tell. But unfortunately her words fell on deaf ears.

It wasn't really that her mother didn't believe her because deep down she knew her little girl was telling the truth. She didn't know how to handle it so she pretended to ignore it, causing Madeline to feel lost and confused. Trying to find a way to escape her pain, Madeline became very promiscuous, rebellious and began to get bad grades in school. She was introduced to drugs and they became her best friend. The drugs kept her distant from people because they just looked at her as a junkie. She was hurting and thought nobody knew. Everything she did was a cry for help. Unfortunately, nobody saw the cry. They only saw the junkie, the crackhead, the whore; but nobody saw the pain.

At a very young age, she learned to hide her pain. Her voice was silent and unless she had a substance controlling her, she was very timid and withdrawn. She didn't know what it meant to be real or to have real love. She wasn't real with herself so how could she be real with anyone else. As she grew to be an adult, she struggled to become who God really called her to be. She didn't even know who that was. Besides, what could God possibly want her to be? If He really wanted her to be something, he would have stopped all the abuse so that she wouldn't have felt like nothing all those years and have to hide in shame.

She heard people talk about how God would give you purpose and show you your gifts. To her, that talk was like a foreign language. She felt that if she could be loved then life would have a new meaning but the sad thing is that she didn't know how to be loved. She thought that being loved was sexual, intimate, and giving someone everything they wanted no matter how bad it hurt her. She felt that if someone loved her that they would want something from her. So Madeline spent most of her life trying to do for others but not wanting others to do for her. She always thought that it would cost her in some way. She would always get hurt because she never felt like the love that she put out was reciprocated. Falling in love with people and giving them her body, but never giving them her heart, not even God.

She spent her life putting up a front and thought she was guarding her heart, but that obviously was not the case. She became angry and bitter. She began hating life and everything that God says it represents. At one point, she became so angry with God that she stopped going to church. Every time she would go to church, it seemed like she was getting another prophecy so she stopped. She didn't want to hear another thing that somebody was telling her that God said.

She thought: *"Lord are you serious, I'm getting all these prophecies about material things and all I really want is for you to tell me that one day my heart will heal. All I need to know is that one day I'll wake up and won't feel the pain. One day I will wake up and won't want to die but will instead feel like there's hope. All I want is to one day feel different than I've ever felt before."*

Madeline's Prayer:

I just want to die! I hate this world, I hate that I was born, I hate my life! I'm stuck in a trap, a cave that is dark. A place where I can see no light. I cover my head and hope that I can hide from the pain, but all I see is what he made me do and what he did to me. All I do is cry and pray that it will all be over soon. I close my eyes and wait for him to finish. I feel so nasty and dirty. I never want anyone to see me again. All I see is ugly. I have to be just as ugly to the world as I am to myself. Everyone is going to think that I am a bad person, that I am dirty, that I am no good. I'm not a bad person, these drugs just keep me numb. They help me not to feel the pain and they make me not care about what people are saying about me. If they want a reason to talk, God I'll give them one, but I'll never let them know what happened to me. No I'll never let them call me dirty and nasty, I would rather they just call me a junky. If I can be honest Lord, I just want to run away, but I don't want to see the outside again. I want to hide, but there's nowhere to go and he'll probably come find me anyway. Can people look at me and see all this dirt? I shower and scrub myself until my skin is raw, but it doesn't take away the dirty feeling. What can I do to be clean? I just can't get clean enough

no matter how hard I try. What did I do to deserve this? Did I put

myself in this position for this to happen? Did I do something to

make him hurt me this way? What would make a grown man want

a little girl? Please God, tell me who was supposed to protect me?

Signed,

Molested Madeline

The Problem ~ One Perspective

There is a time in life when a person can become so hurt and bitter because of the things that have happened to them. They don't understand the reason that life has happened so they attempt to take life in their own hands to protect themselves from being hurt again. They don't understand the reason why things have happened this way. Therefore, they do more damage to themselves because they are unable to release what has happened to them and they believe that they are what has happened to them. This can cause them to hold on to the hurt and suffer in silence, which will inwardly cause more pain. They don't realize that their body is the temple for God to dwell in so they continue to allow themselves to be abused and continue to abuse themselves in the process.

There are times when the pain is so deep, you allow yourself to go into the deepest hole imaginable. Times when you feel that you are not good enough and you can never be anything because of what someone has told you or because of what someone has done to you. Do you know that God will use what you have been through to help someone else and make you better in the process? He can clean you up and purify you so that people cannot even see what you've been through. Some people have to come crawling to God after life has torn them apart. Don't allow the pain to cause your heart to be filthy and do more damage or take you to a place that is hard for you to return from. The further you go, the harder it is to get back to the place that you need to be.

The Solution ~ Another Perspective

When you are going through tough times, it is hard to see the light at the end of the tunnel. You condemn yourself because of the way that you feel and you can't seem to recover from the hurt. There are times when no one can get you out, but you. Times when you have to muster up enough strength to know that you are better than this. In 1 Samuel 30:6, the bible says that "***And David was greatly distressed; for the people spoke of stoning him, because the soul of all the people was grieved,*** *every man for his sons and for his daughters; but David encouraged himself in the Lord his God.*" This was one of the worst times in David's life. David had lost much and didn't know how to recover.

In verse 4, it says: "*Then David and the people that were with him lifted up their voice and wept, until they had no more power to weep.*" In other words, they had cried until they couldn't cry any more. They had lost everything that they felt was important to them and there may be times in our lives when we feel that there's no hope. Times when we feel that it is better to let go than to hold on. Times that you may want to lay down and die. But God has created you with a purpose, with destiny that must be fulfilled. No matter how you may feel, there is a pushing and pulling on the inside that won't allow you to stop.

Understand and know that at this point, you can not go alone. You must do as it says in Proverbs 3:5-6: "*Trust in the Lord with all thine heart; and lean not unto thine own understanding. 6. In all thy ways acknowledge him, and he shall direct thy paths*". I know you know how difficult this must have been for David. He was fighting a battle and trusting God. Yet he felt that he had lost. I'm sure he wanted to blame God for all that had happened but the bible says in verse 8 that: "*David enquired at the Lord, saying, Shall I pursue?"* At this point in our lives we have to let go of everything that we are feeling and go back to God.

You can read the story in 1 Samuel 30 but for now, understand that when we go with God and trust him, no matter what you have lost, you can recover. David was able to recover it all and rescue his wives out of captivity. You too can recover whatever the enemy has taken! God has given you everything you need to make it on this journey and what He has for you is for you. Don't allow situations and circumstances to rob you. Don't hurt yourself more because you can't let go of the pain that someone else has caused. Let them know that what they did to you didn't stop God's plan for you. Romans 8:1, says: *"There is therefore now no condemnation to them which are in Christ Jesus, who walk not after the flesh, but after the Spirit."* Know that what happened to you does not make you who you are, but rather what you do with what has happened to you. God does not condemn you for the actions that someone else has performed, but instead, He judges you by your actions.

He looks at what you do with the life that He has given you, even when someone has hurt you and made you feel that you can't recover. Don't be afraid to encourage yourself, stand up and face your enemy, you can't lay down. No matter how difficult it may be (and it will be difficult) put on the whole armor and ask God the question. Shall I pursue and when He tells you to pursue, go and recover it all!

Hurting People Hurt People, But God HEALS ALL Wounds...

The pain that Madeline was feeling from her abuse made her act out in ways that she had never done before. Yes it's true, she was hurting from the abuse, but because she didn't know how to let go of the hurt, she was holding on to the pain. On the inside, Madeline felt ashamed and therefore, she allowed the shame to make her feel condemned and guilty. She didn't know what the guilt was about because she didn't believe that she had done anything wrong, but on the other hand maybe she did. Maybe she was wrong for not telling. She was so concerned about how people would look at her if they knew.

She was embarrassed because she had let this happen to her. How embarrassing is it for people to know that you were so weak that you allowed someone to violate you? What would people say about you? Did you want this to happen? Of course not, but they are not going to see that because you didn't tell anyone when it was taking place. Afterall, who were you supposed to tell? How much confusion would telling cause anyway and who was it going to help? Yes, it may have relieved her, but it would have hurt so many others in the process.

Madeline was just a little girl but her innocence was taken away from her and things would never go back to the way they used to be. So therefore, she just kept her mouth shut and kept it to herself, but she grew up hurting and continued to hold on to the pain. Holding on to the pain caused her to hurt others. She had a baby at a young age due to being promiscuous. Unfortunately, she didn't know who the father was. Instead of giving the baby up for adoption to someone that could love and nurture her, she kept the baby and passed on the abuse.

She didn't know how to be a mother so she thought that the baby was just a trophy. As the baby grew up and began to show traits of her mother, Madeline became abusive. She didn't know how to help her child so she would leave the child when times were tough. Or she would go out to get drugs and would bring men home to use the child as payment for her habits. Unfortunately, because of Madeline's pain, the child was abused and the cycle continued. The child grew up and became just like her mother.

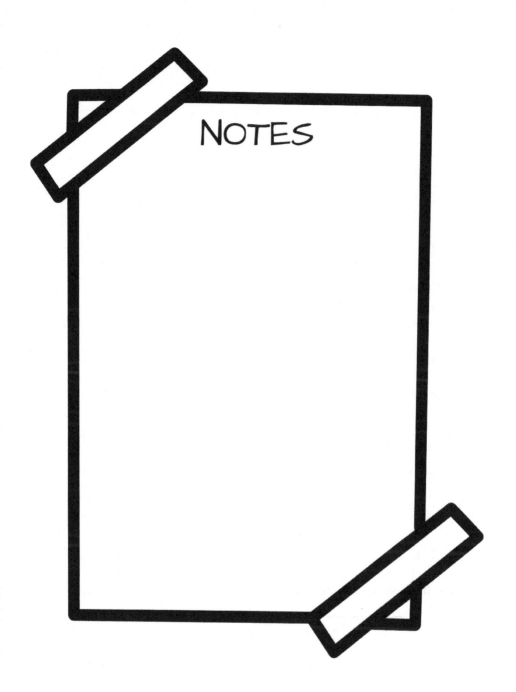

NOTES

Chapter 5 - Ethan's Story

Looking from the Outside

*E*than was a very quiet and subtle guy. He had very few friends

and the few friends that he did have, he kept very close. He pretty much

stayed to himself unless he was hanging out with his family or friends.

That was his life: work, his family and his friends. He worked hard and

he loved hard. He loved hanging with his people so when those close to

him began to leave this world Ethan didn't handle it very well. It

appeared that family members and his closest friends were leaving one

after the other. In a span of three years, Ethan lost several people that

were very significant in his life.

That's not to say that those who were left weren't important

because they were. It's just that these were the ones that he leaned on and

depended on, maybe even too much. These were some of the ones he

could go to for anything when he needed it. Oh stop! Don't judge Ethan

too hard, at some point, you have probably experienced the same thing.

Instead of trusting God for the answers, you run to your friends for

advice first. Whether right or wrong, everyone has probably depended on somebody way too much. Now, because Ethan didn't know how to handle his grief and his losses, he held all his pain inside and became very angry with God. Ethan questioned God and wondered why he was taking everyone that was close to him.

Not only did Ethan question God, he questioned himself and his relationship with God. He felt that there must have been something that he was doing wrong. How do you lose family and friends all at the same time? Although he knew he really had nothing to do with God's plan of life and death and His choice to call his people home, he still became angry and blamed God. He didn't know how he was going to make it. Every time he thought he was allowing himself to grieve and heal, someone else would die. It became a cycle that he couldn't process and because he was angry with God. He felt that he couldn't go to him, which means he also cut off his communication, connection and relationship with God.

Therefore, he just held all his feelings inside and threw himself into his work. He became even more introverted. This didn't help Ethan to process what was taking place. Every time someone else would die, every death resurfaced and caused him to be even more numb. He didn't know what was happening in his life so when he wasn't working, he was home under the covers depressed. No one even knew what he was going through, or so he thought.

Ethan's Prayer:

I cannot believe this has happened again! How many people have to die, God are you serious? Are you just taking everyone in my life away from me? What am I going to do? I have no one and nothing to live for. How am I supposed to live in this world without the ones I love? I mean I know I still have people left and please don't think that I'm not grateful for those that are left. It just seems that there is more with you than there is with me. I know you give life and you have the right to take it away. I know we all have a date and an appointed time. I know you love them and they belong to you, but I wasn't prepared for this and I just need some time to process it all. The emptiness and void that I feel is unbearable. This cycle seems to continue and it seems to be never-ending. I don't know how much longer I can't take this and the pain is not fading away. Every time I think I'm beginning to be able to move forward and accept one, then another one is gone. God don't you see this is too much pain!?

Signed,

Empty Ethan

The Problem ~ One Perspective

Although death is a part of life it still can take us by surprise. It may not be that it's a surprise but most people just don't think it's going to happen to them. Or at least they feel like they have time to do what they want to do at their own pace. People think that they have forever. Forever to get it right, forever to waste time, forever to do this and forever to do that. They put off serving God and feel like they can get to him just when they need him.

The bible says: "*And as it is appointed unto men once to die, but after this the judgment.*" (Hebrews 9:27, KJV) So why must procrastination be a part of the norm? For some there is no urgency to do what God says to do and before you know it, time has slipped away and your age has increased. The body is slowing down and you can't do what you used to do. You must do what you can with the strength that you have left and pray that God will have mercy for your latter years. At this point, you begin to complain because you say it has caught you by surprise and now you have a bucket list. You're trying to get it all done, but you don't have the strength that you used to have.

What about all those years that were spent on just being you and thinking you had forever. Now you wish you could get them back, but you can't. *"You who are young, make the most of your youth. Relish your youthful vigor. Follow the impulses of your heart. If something looks good to you, pursue it. But know also that not just anything goes; You have to answer to God for every last bit of it."* (Ecclesiastes 11: 9-10, MSG) So yes, enjoy life and have fun; but don't forget God. Do what you can to prepare for it and prepare others around you. Christ had to die in order for one to live and one must die in order to meet Him and live eternally.

The Solution ~ Another Perspective

You cannot allow those that have gone before you to cause you to not want to live for the glory of God. You see there is nothing wrong with grieving the loss of a loved one, but at some point, you have to understand that God doesn't make mistakes. Everyone must understand that they have been put here with a purpose and once they have fulfilled that purpose, their work on earth is done and they return to the Heavenly Father.

The bible says **in 2 Corinthians 5:8: "to be absent from the body is to be present with the Lord."** Therefore, if your loved ones were living the promised life of God then you will see them again. They are not lost, but are waiting for the reunion for you to join them when your work down here is done. Think of it like this: Remember the days when mothers and fathers would go off work and children would go to school? Everyone would look forward to coming home and eating dinner together?

I know we don't see that as much as we used to but during those times everyone would be excited to come back home together after being away from each other all day. That's how it is in the kingdom of God when someone leaves this earth, they retire and their work is done. No matter what that age, we have to keep on working. Those of us that are left here on earth will one day reach full retirement age. No one except God is privy to that information, but when the day comes, we get to retire and join our loved ones for the biggest feast ever. We can't stop working because God is working out some good things in our life. Things that we can't even imagine or think about.

Not grieving is just like not breathing. It literally sucks the life out of you. Imagine someone holding their hand over your mouth and not allowing you to breathe. You want to scream, but you can't. You want to let it all out, but instead you have to hold it all in because their hand is covering your mouth. You eventually lose consciousness or they remove their hand to allow you to freely breathe. That is what it's like *not* to grieve. You hold it all in until finally you pass out from exhaustion or you eventually open yourself up to trust God and others to help you through this process. One may think that because they are not feeling the need to express grief outwardly that they are dealing with things and managing properly. But that is not always the case.

As you may already know, grieving comes with several stages and no matter how long it may take you to go through those stages, it is necessary to go through them in order or grieve in a healthy manner. Skipping stages may actually prevent the healing process because you stay stuck in one or many of the processes without completing them.

Let's look at the 7 stages of grief, as I had to learn about when I was going through this process. 1.) **Shock and disbelief denial** – The phase of unbelief. The place where you can't believe this is happening, especially when a person may not be sick or it happens suddenly. 2.) **Denial** – In this place, you are probably not dealing with reality or trying to deny that the death even occurred, even though you know it has. 3.) **Bargaining** – This may bring about a lot of the "what ifs" or trying to make deals with God so that you can get through. 4.) **Guilt** – You may feel a sense of responsibility or tell yourself that you should have done something different. This stage is where you may be the hardest on yourself and even beat yourself up the most. 5.) **Anger** – These feelings and emotions may be directed at God, the person or whomever you feel is the cause. 6.) **Depression** – Feelings of anxiety can sometimes become unbearable and often require professional help, if in this state too long. 7.) **Acceptance and hope** – The place that you want to be.

It is not determined how long a person may be in any one particular stage because everyone is different. However, the goal is to go through it and not to avoid it. If you try to avoid it, you will eventually come back to it and it can also prolong your healing process. You see God is so wise that when He created man, He created the body to respond to the processes that you go through in life. Therefore, the body has a way of responding to grief, if you allow this process in a healthy manner. The thing is that God was preparing us but we didn't prepare ourselves. When we go through the stages of grief properly, our body will respond to the pain and the void that we feel and adjust in its own way to this normal process. When you prepare yourself and trust God through this process, it will relieve your body the way that God intended for it to.

No matter how much people try, they ***cannot*** determine your grieving process. Don't let people tell you how long you are supposed to grieve! People will try to tell you what your grieving process is supposed to be when they don't even know what their own process is supposed to be. Every individual has to determine that for themselves and your grief process won't be the same for everyone that you grieve in your life. Although you go through the same stages of grief for every loss, you will not grieve every loss the same way. Losing a spouse is very different from losing a friend and losing a child is very different from losing a parent. Same stages of grief, different process, timing and response.

Hurting People Hurt People, But God HEALS ALL Wounds…
Wow this is a big one…

Allow me to be very transparent with this subject because this is one where the devil tried to take me out but to God be the glory for the great things He has done! In 2009, death became a bit different for me. It was different when my Godmother passed away and then in 2010 when my husband went into the hospital. I had experienced people that were close to me dying before, but for some reason death began to look different or maybe I began to realize that it could be me. My Godmother had been sick for some years but because I couldn't face her being sick, I avoided seeing her. I felt as if that were going to stop anything from happening. Instead, it robbed me of the time that I could have spent with her. Anyway, I would talk to her on the phone but whenever she asked me to come to visit, I found a reason not to.

I wouldn't face the fact that I was afraid to see her in that state so I avoided it. Instead of facing the pain while she was alive, I had to face it as I watched them roll her out in the casket. I beat myself up for the longest and regretted the fact that I hadn't gone to visit. She was there for me whenever I needed her but yet I was too afraid to face her during the times that she needed me most. I thought I would never forgive myself for that and repetitively asked God to help me to get through the pain in hopes that I would never experience it again. Well after getting through that, a few months later, my husband was in a horrible car accident and was in the hospital. Thank God he made it out, but not long after, my brother in law, who was also my Pastor, became very ill.

Needless to say, 2010 was a very challenging year and it wasn't over yet. We still had two months to go and were definitely praying that the year ended much better than it came in but that wasn't the case. Yes, my Pastor was released and was able to once again walk through the church doors and we knew we had the victory. It was like after being in a year-long war and finally being able to declare that you had won. Oh, we danced, shouted, and praised God all over that church. I'm sure that was a good thing because little did we know, God was refueling us for the next task. Amongst the many works that my Pastor had to finish, I always said God raised him up to help me to face the unimaginable that was about to come.

December brought in a beast that rendered me powerless. I will never forget the call and hearing my Pastor on the other end saying, "Minister Neet, you need to come home." It didn't sound good at all. But what else could be happening? Surely things can't be any worse than they had already been. After all, God had just brought us through the rainstorms and the snow blizzards of life, right? Well, I arrived at my house and had to call the paramedics. I won't go into the specifics of how we got here, but I will say that it wasn't a pleasant ride.

From December 12, 2010 to January 30, 2011 my husband lay in a coma and I never heard his voice again. Now although this was painful, I was able to look back and realize how merciful God was. I realized how on the exact date the previous year, he was in that horrible car accident and God could have taken him then. But instead, He gave us another whole year together. Not only that, my daughter was supposed to be with him on that day, but due to some other events, we changed plans, which would have created an even more horrific scenario.

Now I will say that what you do with the time that God gives you is up to you. We had just celebrated (or not celebrated) our ten-year anniversary and we definitely didn't think it would be our last. For some reason, this year, we did nothing spectacular to commemorate the moment. It was just another anniversary to us and after all, we loved each other and we could do things together anytime or so we thought. Sometimes in loving one another, you just don't always make a big deal of things, but now I question…Would we have made a big deal if we knew it was our last? Now after I beat myself up about not visiting my Godmother, you would think that I would have learned my lesson. To be really honest, my husband and I were arguing about something and chose to go separate ways on that anniversary. The sad thing is after he was gone, it seemed so small that I couldn't even remember what we argued about. Afterall, whatever it was, it could have been fixed while he was alive, but not now. I'm just saying there are times when we may not think we take people for granted but we also don't celebrate them like we should. Do we really give them their flowers while they can smell them, or do we end up with a bunch of regrets after they are gone?

Now as if this wasn't enough, after 3 months had passed, while on my way to my grandfather's funeral, I received a call that my mother-in-law had passed. I thought Lord, not another year like this! Unfortunately, this was yet another challenging year and besides all that I was trying to finish up all the parties that my dear husband had scheduled and received deposits for. Thanks to the wonderful staff that he had working with him, we were able to get them all done. I was keeping myself busy and my body was acting like nothing had happened until the day came and it hit me. The day that we said "I do" is now "no more" because I did until death.

Wow! If I could only go back, what would I do differently? Well I would have spent the anniversary differently that's for sure, but I couldn't focus on that. No, there was the house to sell, the demands of being a single parent and so many other things on my plate now. My life had totally been turned upside down in a matter of moments. Yet, I still knew that God was keeping me because I hadn't gone and crawled up in a corner. Yes, there were definitely times that I wanted to do just that but I had a little girl to raise. She had already lost one parent so she definitely couldn't lose another. So just when I thought I was about to be back on my feet, that dreadful 4th weekend in January rolled around. The fact that we were going to repeat the same events that we had dealt with the previous year had never crossed my mind and this time it was a double whammy!

Both my aunt and my brother-in-law/Pastor, were both in the hospital facing the same outcome. I thought we would make it through, but here I was again not able to face what the possibilities might be. Unfortunately, we spent the 2nd year doing the same thing we had just done at the same time the previous year. I remember thinking, this is unbelievable. Is this Deja Vu? God what is your reason for this and what in the heck is going on? At this point I had given up, I couldn't take the thought of death anymore. I decided to go live with my grandmother for a while and be around her loving smile and comfort that I knew she would give.

I needed some light to shine on all this darkness and I knew there was nobody like my "Grand!" I just loved being in her presence and I knew that when I was around her, I was in the presence of God. I spent the next year trying to get myself together and thought that this transition was good for both me and my daughter. Life was beginning to look up and I was almost feeling normal again. Besides the daily drives from Harford County, MD to Baltimore County, MD; life was not too bad and God gave me the strength I needed every day.

But the closer we came to December, the more anxiety and fear I felt. While others were excited for the holidays and the new year to come, I was dreading it. The past two years were a living hell and this time I was really afraid of that dreadful 4th weekend in January. This time when I got the call, I thought I had faith. I prayed all the way home and I knew everything would be fine. I wasn't going to accept that we would deal with another tragedy but when I got to the house, the grandmother that I had just had dinner with the night before was surrounded by those in tears waiting for the mortician to arrive to remove her cold body.

I was so mad with God I didn't know what to do. How in the world could He take my "Grand"? What was His purpose? Was He just trying to make me suffer? Then suddenly I came to my senses and I realized that she wasn't mine. She belonged to God and more than anything she lived wholeheartedly for Him. She longed to be with Him, but of course that didn't stop my heart from breaking and this time it was shattered into pieces that I thought would never mend. I thought that my heart was too broken to feel pain again until in 2015 when one of my best

84

girlfriend's lost the fight to cancer and then in 2017 cancer took my "PIPSIL" too.

If you're wondering why I decided to share my story here it is. I thought this was the last draw. The enemy wanted to kill me through God choosing to take His children home. Just as they had left I wanted to leave and I often had thoughts of how it could happen. I was so heartbroken and distraught that I thought I had nothing to live for. Even though I had to raise my daughter, there were times that I thought she would be better off with someone else because I didn't think I could give her what she needed. I felt that I was too broken to help anyone.

I knew I had done some messed up things and I truly thought God was punishing me in the most tormenting way. I thought that things would never get better and every day I woke up wishing that I didn't. I used to ask God why did He wake me up to torment me more? You see, I had the wrong perspective and I was looking at things the wrong way. The death of my loved ones was causing me to hurt me. Because I didn't know how to grieve, I chose to do it in unhealthy ways, which eventually affected my health and caused me to no longer dream and believe that I had a purpose to fulfill. I had no plan for the future and I was hurting myself with bad thoughts and bad actions, basically committing a slow suicide. I wasn't living, I was merely surviving to get through life the best way I knew how. I was always depressed and sad, but didn't want others to see my pain. What appeared to be okay on the outside was a horrible wreck on the inside.

Others Gone in the midst of these writings, but never forgotten:
Pastor Mayo Brown (aunt),
Pastor Almeter Diggs (mother-in-law),
Quinlin Diggs (sister-in-law),
Dr. Stanley Diggs (previous pastor and brother-in-law),
Charles Frazier (dad),
Shirley Hamilton (aunt)
Nonni Jenkins (forever friend),
Elbert Moody (grandfather).

Cousins
Kevin Brown
Dorothea Harmon
Gerald Hynson
Nikki Ward

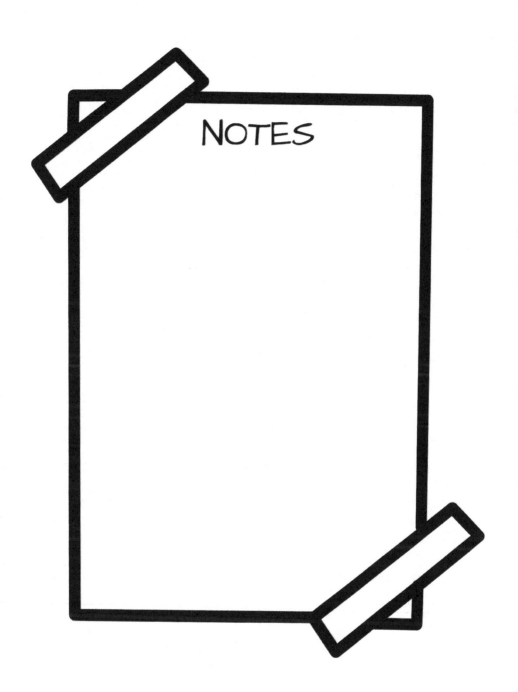

NOTES

Chapter 6 – Grace's Story

Cleaning Up the Clutter: Coming Out of the Mess

Looking from the Outside

Finally, it was time to move to another home but Grace had so

much junk and clutter that had piled up over the years. It seemed

impossible for her to get things boxed and ready to go. Every time she

would think about picking up the pieces and packing, it made her tired.

She looked around and the piles of clothes and all the stuff that had

accumulated was overwhelming. The boxes made her exhausted as they

sat there just looking for her to do something with them. Of course, she

had no choice but to pack them because the marriage that she depended

on was over. She couldn't take his lying and cheating anymore. No

matter how she tried to ignore it, it was just hurting her more and more.

He was so arrogant, so full of himself, and he knew that she needed him

for support.

He did what he wanted to do, with whomever he chose to do it

with and he no longer tried to hide it from her. So, for years Grace

drowned in her sorrows and for years the clothes just continued to pile

up. Every day when she went into her house, she went straight to bed to avoid looking at all the junk around her. Each day she just ignored the obvious and each day she became more and more depressed. Before she knew it, she stopped inviting people over because she was tired of making excuses for the way things looked. It took more than one day for all the clutter to get there and it was surely going to take more than one day for the clutter to be removed.

Grace's Prayer:

God,

I know it's been years since I've talked to you, but I know my grandmother said that you are able to do all things, but fail. You have been the God of my grandmother as long as I can remember and I never saw her lack for anything. I remember she used to say, "God I acknowledge you and know that you will direct my path". She called you a heart fixer and a minder regulator. God she also said you were the wheel in the middle of the wheel. Now I never knew what any of that meant and still don't. But one thing I remembered was when times were the toughest she would say that you would never leave us nor forsake us. God I know I haven't done the best with my life and I haven't always made the best decisions. I've tried to live on my own and I know I've put many things before you. I've allowed stuff to comfort me and not your

Holy Spirit and I've tried to do things on my own. Now I'm asking

you to forgive me and help me to do things your way. Please be

my God and my Savior. Regulate my mind and fix my heart from

all the hurt and pain that I feel. Take control of my life and lead

me to a place with you that I have never been before. I'm grateful

that you have kept me up to this point, but I promise if you teach

me how to live for you, I will tell others of your goodness and live

a life that is pleasing to you. Help me Father to be the best

version of me that I can be.

Signed,

Grateful Grace

The Problem ~ One Perspective

Cleaning up clutter is sometimes the hardest thing to do. It appears that it's a whole lot quicker and easier to create a mess than it is to clean up that same mess. Truth is, it takes just as long to make the mess as it does to clean it up. After a long day of work, sometimes the first thing you want to do is get out of your clothes and get comfortable. But is being comfortable really comfortable if it's going to cause you discomfort later? It's one thing to come home from a long day at the office and take off your clothes to get comfortable, but it's a whole different thing to remove those clothes, drop them on the floor day after day, only to realize that in your getting comfortable, you have created a pile that will take you as much time to pick up as it did to put down.

That same pile that it took you a month to create, you want it to be gone in a day. Sometimes a person can want good results without developing good habits and unfortunately, one can want to get out of a thing much quicker than it took them to get in it. Likewise, there are situations that an individual can get themselves into through being habitually disobedient, but then want God to get them out of it instantaneously. Just because it's possible to microwave food, doesn't mean that this process of cooking will give you the best source of nutrition. Sometimes God delivers you immediately and sometimes He allows you to go through a process. It doesn't mean that the work has not begun, it just means that God is saying that this one has to be slow cooked and not microwaved in order to ensure the best nutritional value.

I'm probably the last one to use analogies in reference to cooking because it's not something I enjoy doing, but I've been around enough good cooks to know that good food takes time. Time to prepare, time to marinate, time to cook and sometimes even time to cool before eating. I remember the days of watching the preparation for the big meals during the holidays or big events. You always knew that the prepping was starting days before.

I never saw the people who were doing the preparation wait until the day of the event to start shopping for ingredients, they always did it in advance. As kids we didn't have to cook, but we definitely had to help with the preparations. We were taught to make sure we had everything we needed before we began. You're probably wondering where I'm going with this, but one of the many things I've learned about God is that He makes all things work together for our good. Everything that we go through is an ingredient that He uses to put us together to make us great. Just as it is with cooking, each ingredient by itself may not taste very good, but when you mix it all in the pot, it creates the perfect meal.

The Solution ~ Another Perspective

Cleaning up clutter requires taking one ingredient or one piece at a time and determining its value. Sometimes that means picking up an item or sometimes that could mean picking up the whole pile and throwing it in the laundry for everything to be washed. But even when the whole pile needs washing, the clothes must first be separated.

Cleaning clutter is never easy, but always necessary in order to go to the next level. The process is not always embraced by an individual, but God always knows what's best. Therefore, we must do our part because He is always going to do His. Just as with cooking, cleaning clutter takes time to prep, time to marinate, time to cook and sometimes time to cool down.

Or in bible terms, time to *"renew your mind"* (Ephesians 4:23), time to accept *"beauty for your ashes"* (Isaiah 61:3), and then time to realize and know that *"all things are working together for your good"* (Romans 8:28). This is all a process and will take time. The time it takes will also depend on what God is trying to teach you and how quickly you adjust or accept the teaching. Either way, trust God and trust His process because no matter what, His way is going to be the best and most effective way. In all of that, once the clutter is clean, don't allow yourself to be so comfortable that you bring in new clutter, but ask God to help you to live a clutter free life. *"Whom the Son has set free is free indeed."* (John 8:36) Walk into your freedom and live in your abundance.

Hurting People Hurt People, But God HEALS ALL Wounds…

You see, Grace was used to people taking care of her and picking up after her all the time. She came from a wealthy home and was the child that disrespected the nanny and told her what to do. She took it for granted that her parents had worked really hard to accumulate their own wealth and although she couldn't realize it at the time, she felt entitled. Unfortunately, at the same time because her parents had very demanding jobs, they had to put in a lot of hours and they didn't have the time to stay home and give her the attention that she needed. Yes, she had everything she wanted, but they showed her love by giving her more stuff and that's what she wanted as she grew up. This caused Grace to always be out at a party, hanging with people that had their nose in the air and dressed themselves in very seductive and revealing attire.

So they were always encountering people with money that just wanted to have a good time for the night. Because of what Grace was used to, she later married a hard-working man that bought her everything she wanted, but spent no time with her. His way of showing her love was giving her more stuff, but he was always on business trips so she spent a lot of time in a big house alone, but now being a married woman, she couldn't just hang in the clubs and enjoy the partying lifestyle. Unfortunately, what she didn't know was that early on in the marriage, he was already cheating on her so while she was sitting in the big house alone, he was out with his mistress.

After many years of betrayal, he became more careless with his lies and affairs so when she found out, she was hurt and heartbroken and eventually the marriage ended in divorce. Soon Grace had to get a job and work, something that she definitely wasn't accustomed to doing. After her divorce, she no longer wanted to live in the big city so she moved to a small town to get away from all the friends that they both knew as a couple. She had to take a job as a waitress because she had no other experience. She didn't get a lot for alimony and of course with all the people that he knew, he basically got away with paying practically nothing because they had no children. Grace tried to hide her pain and start her life over, but although she could hide her feelings when she was around other people, she couldn't hide her pain when she came home. Therefore, the clutter just grew and grew and grew!

Until one day Grace decided she could not do the pity party any longer. She had to decide to pick herself up, dust herself off and be the big girl that she felt deep down on the inside that she could be. Growing up her grandmother would take her to church, so she knew a bit about God, but had no relationship with him at all. One thing Grace knew was that she couldn't do this alone so she decided that she would try this God that her grandmother was always praying to.

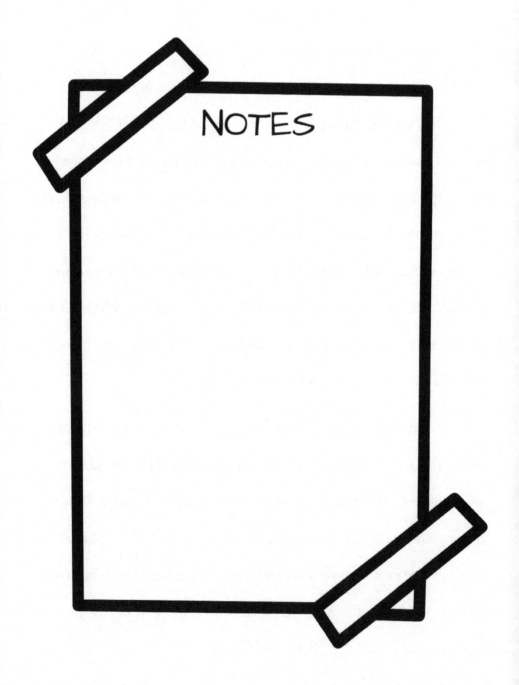

NOTES

Chapter 7- Olivia's Story

Be Still: Dealing with God

Looking from the Outside

*O*livia, Olivia, Olivia. Well, Olivia was trying and thought she

was doing all of the right things. She was spending daily time with God,

reading her Bible, going to Bible study regularly and was at the church

every time the doors were open. From a spiritual aspect, everyone

thought Olivia had it all together. She would give to the poor, feed the

homeless and even do a couple mission trips every year. Olivia wasn't

intentionally working hard to try to win God over. She just thought these

were the things she was supposed to do, but in her heart, she was

constantly questioning God, feeling angry and holding grudges. In only

focusing on what she thought she was supposed to do, there was no

balance in her life. She was as they say: "so heavenly bound, but no

earthly good". She felt like everyone else was having fun and she was

always busy working and doing something for somebody else.

She thought that she was doing what God wanted her to do but

she felt like she just wasn't getting anywhere and there was always a

void. Everyone was getting showers of blessings, except her. Everyone else seemed happy but she had to pretend to be happy. Everything she was praying for was going to someone else or so she thought. Guess she never realized that what God has for her is for her and no one can take it from her. But yet she still kept doing and she stayed frustrated and she kept feeling like all the blessings were just passing her by. Funny thing about Olivia is that she would dare not tell anybody that she was upset with God, not even God, but of course He already knew. It wasn't until Olivia became so devastated that she had a heart attack that she was able to be still and realize how out of balance her life was.

Olivia's Prayer:

God help me to understand your will for my life. I know you can do the impossible, like move mountains and raise folks from the dead, but all I ask for is small simple things and it seems like everybody else is getting blessed but me. What am I doing wrong, why do I still feel a void in my life when I feel like I'm trying to do the best I can? When is my turn coming? I'm not trying to be selfish or self-righteous. I know you love me, but it seems like you are showing love to everyone, but me. I mean I'm not trying to tell you what to do Lord, but some of these people you bless are doing everything, but serving you. I'm trying to live right most days and

yet my blessings seem to be held up in a cloud or something.

Please God just help me to fill this emptiness inside. If I'm not

doing right, help me to get it right. I just want to know that you

haven't left me.

Signed,

One Blessing Will Do, Olivia

The Problem ~ One Perspective

My God, My God, why hast thou forsaken me? Have you ever
had that thought? You feel like you're trying to do all of the right things.
Are you trying to do it in your own power and in your own might? Are
your behaviors just habits that you have formed and your life is just on
auto pilot because you've been doing the same thing for so long, but you
are no longer doing it from the heart. Have you ever felt like God wasn't
hearing you or definitely wasn't talking to you? Are there moments that it
just seems that God is being quiet and He doesn't have anything to say?

He's still speaking, you are just not hearing because you are
focused on what you are naturally used to doing without thinking about
what you're doing. There is a time in life where you just need to be still.

Psalm 46:10 says, "***Be still and know that I am God***". There is a time that God has to make you be still. This became real for all in March of 2020, when the world was hit with the COVID-19 pandemic. The world was still, but all thought that it was only for a moment. Even people that were in their 80s and 90s reported that they had never encountered anything like this in their lifetime. Bodies were being bagged and people were dying by the thousands and couldn't even have a proper burial. People were afraid to be around their loved ones, afraid of what they would get or even what they would transmit.

Graduations, proms and social gatherings were being canceled. There were no more get-togethers with your friends for food and fun; and if you didn't get along with the people you lived with, you were in big trouble. Surely this thing would not last long. Soon offices will reopen and employees will be back to work and things will be back to normal. Unfortunately, this was not the case. Offices were closed for months and everyone was working from home, which became the new norm. After two years of working from home some employees had still not returned to work and many had to change careers, their lifestyles and many learned to become entrepreneurs. Yes, the world became still and it appeared that God was talking and for once almost everybody was listening.

The Solution ~ Another Perspective

In living up to an image and only doing what you think you are supposed to do, there is no balance in your life. You think you are pleasing God, but you're not. You're not doing it from the heart and you're mad and angry with everybody while you're doing it because you think that you're doing all the work and everybody else is getting all the blessings. There's a story in Luke 10, that speaks of the two sisters of Lazarus, whose names were Martha and Mary. Martha was focused on the wrong things, while Mary was focused on Jesus. However, Martha had an issue, she was upset because she felt that she was doing all the work and Mary was resting and having all the fun.

Jesus spoke to Martha in verse 41-42 and said: "*Martha, Martha, thou art careful and troubled about many things: (v. 41) But one thing is needful: and Mary has chosen that good part, which shall not be taken away from her." (v.42)* In other words, Jesus was saying to Martha, be still, you're focusing on the wrong things. Mary is choosing to focus on spending time with me and that's more important because what she is getting is going to be with her forever. Sometimes God is saying your focus is in the wrong direction and you need to make a shift. Colossians 3:2, says: *"Set your affections on things above, not on things on the earth."* Work is a way of life, one must work in order to live, but you also cannot fulfill purpose without spending time with God. God wants you to be healed, whole and complete in Him. He wants you to live life in abundance. So even in the moments when it feels like God is not talking, He is, you just need to be still and take time to listen.

Although there are times when it seems difficult, be still! You can't always go by what we see or feel, sometimes, you just have to know. Know that God is there, know that *"God will not leave you or forsake you."* (Deuteronomy 31:6, NIV) Know that God will be true to His word. Stand on what He has told you in the past and trust Him. Especially if you are trying to believe in God for a promise. These times can be most difficult because one of the hardest things to do in life is to wait when you feel like you're not getting any results. It is in these times that you must stand on what you know and use the word that is on the inside and continue to rehearse the word and recite it and study it and believe it. You can't give up, no matter how long it takes. Know that God is God! Your faith may want to waver, but trust God and know that *"He is not slack concerning His promise."* (2 Peter 3:9)

Have you ever felt like Olivia? Have you felt like you were doing everything you thought you should, but God wasn't hearing you or talking to you? Are there moments that it just seems that God is being quiet and He doesn't have anything to say? Can we admit that sometimes having to wait on God causes us pain and grief because in that moment we don't understand what God is doing? At that moment, we don't know why God is not answering our prayers. If we could be honest with ourselves, it makes us feel that God is neglecting us or punishing us for some reason. Can we admit that sometimes we even feel that God is hurting us?

We feel that we are being led by the spirit, but those things that we are believing in don't happen the way we expect them to. How do we respond to feeling that we are hurt by God? Do we shut Him out? Do we stop praying? Do we stay home from church? The responses may be different for us all but it is true that we do have a response whether it be verbal or nonverbal. Unfortunately, most of us feel that we can't show that we are angry with God or tell Him how we feel so we act out as if God doesn't know what we're doing. The truth is God knows all and He sees all even when we feel that we have been hurt by Him. Sometimes in the moments that we feel that we are not getting any responses, it's because we are doing too much. Our focus is not in the right place and God is trying to get our attention and change our direction. Know that His word is His voice and God is just saying, "Be still".

Sometimes we have a lot going on or we're trying to fill so many roles that we can be all over the place. But God wants us to be still. With all that's going on in the world, quiet time and meditation is necessary. It can be a good way to relax your body and your mind. When meditating, remember to meditate on His word. Recall those promises that He has given and know that sometimes waiting is just a part of the process. It's not God's way of punishing you, it's His way of showing you how much He loves you. Just as you wouldn't give your children what you know they can't handle, God will not give you what you're not ready for. So, as it is said in Philippians 4:8: "*Finally, brethren, whatsoever things are true, whatsoever things are honest, whatsoever things are just, whatsoever things are pure, whatsoever things are lovely, whatsoever things are of good report; if there be any virtue, and if there be any praise, think on these things".* For it is when thinking on these things

that God is able to speak to us and allow us to rest in Him.

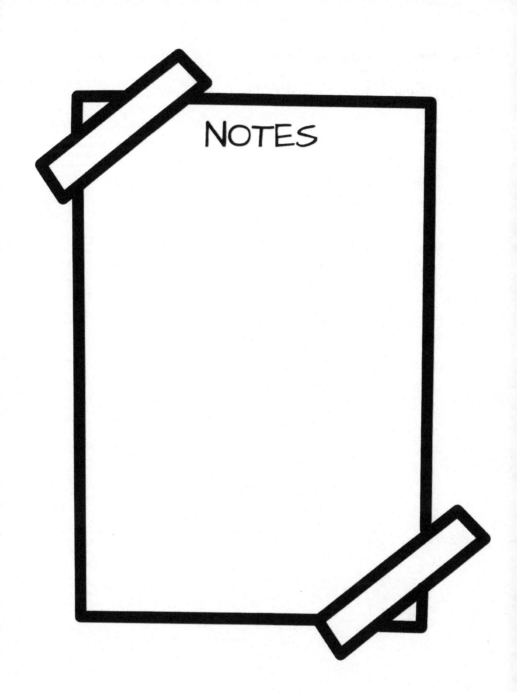

NOTES

Chapter 8 - DeMarco's Story

It Wasn't Easy, But It Was Worth It: Restoration

Looking from the Outside

DeMarco had been through so much in his life. His mom was

shot in front of him by a stray bullet when he was just six years old. His

dad died after struggling for years with mental illness when DeMarco

was fourteen years old. He was able to stay with his grandmother until

she died a couple years later when he was sixteen. From the age of 16,

DeMarco was in foster homes until he was eighteen years old. Due to his

anger and aggressive behaviors, he went from one home to another.

Every home he was in, he found some way to self-sabotage so that he

didn't have to stay. Being on the streets, he hooked up with the wrong

crowd and he began to be in gangs, carrying guns and selling drugs.

At the age of 22, DeMarco went to jail and got a ten-year

sentence for being in the wrong place at the wrong time. He didn't do the

crime but was caught on the scene and refused to snitch on his buddies.

Being in jail gave DeMarco plenty of time to think about the lifestyle that

he had chosen to live. He had been raised in the church by his

grandmother and couldn't understand why he allowed himself to go in the direction that he did. He realized how the death of his mother, father and grandmother had affected his life. He also realized that he could have made better choices.

He began to speak with a therapist and also began to attend Bible study while in jail. After seven years, he went up for parole and was released on probation. After being released, he joined a local church and began to help with the youth in the community. DeMarco was able to help a lot of the gang members to turn to God and became a big brother to many young boys on the streets because of his story.

DeMarco's Prayer:

Father,

I know I don't deserve your love because of the many things that I have done, but I know you still love me and you want the best for me. I know you sent your Son to die for me so I ask for your forgiveness. Help me to get on the right path, help me to be better in this life and be an example for others. I was taught the right things to do and even though I got on the wrong track, I know that you are a forgiving God. So, I'm crying out for your help. Allow me to use the dangerous life that I have lived to keep others out of danger. Allow me to make a difference in a child's life before they go in the direction that I was going. Help me to not be ashamed to tell my story, but to help others to change their lives when they see what I have been through. I know you didn't create me to do the things that I'm doing, so show me how to be a blessing to others and teach them how to start out on the journey knowing that there is a God that loves them no matter what they go through. Teach me Lord and I will teach others. Thank you for your grace and mercy, without you I would have never been restored!

Signed,

Determined DeMarco

The Problem ~ One Perspective

There are many times when youth are exposed to situations that they have to live with for the rest of their lives. Most scars are formed at a very young age. Sometimes they see more than they need to and depending on the life inside the household, things can be more dysfunctional than anyone on the outside may ever know. There are times that children may go to school on an empty stomach or may have been up all night because they are living in the house with an abusive parent. Sometimes there are no signs of what is going on at home but then sometimes there are. Kids can become very rebellious and defiant trying to deal with what is taking place in the house.

Truth is, children are not supposed to have to deal with adult situations. Unfortunately, it can also be the parents that are causing stress on the child by trying to make them their friend and telling them things that a child should not have to know or ever have to deal with. According to the U. S Department of Justice and a study of a national sample of American children, 60 percent were exposed to violence, crime, or abuse in their homes, schools, and communities. Almost 40 percent of American children were direct victims of 2 or more violent acts, and 1 in 10 were victims of violence 5 or more times.

Almost 1 in 10 American children saw one family member assault another family member, and more than 25 percent had been exposed to family violence during their life. (ojp.gov) This means that children are being exposed in the environments that they are living in on a daily basis and therefore, the impact is going to be greater because it is among those that they are familiar with. People say that children are resilient and this may be true about some things, but children are also very impressionable so they also repeat what they see.

The Solution ~ Another Perspective

When it comes to restoration, you must acknowledge your wrong and renew your mind. Restoration can only be accomplished by repenting, trusting God and allowing Him to have full control. Romans 12: 1-2 says: *"**Therefore be not conformed to this world, but be ye transformed by the renewing of your mind"***. Renewing the mind can be one of the most difficult, but rewarding decisions a person can make. First of all, when a person decides that they are going to renew their mind, they must realize that it must be done daily and it's not just a one-time event.

Every day, you must make the decision to live right because every day, the enemy is determined to make you live wrong. This is a daily walk with God and is something that you will be doing for the rest of your life. However, restoration can begin the moment that you make the choice that you are tired of being the way that you are and that you want to make a change.

Restoration will push you to birth a new journey because you don't want to go back to what you were doing before.

There was a song by the Winans many years ago called "Restoration", a part of the lyrics said: *"What would I know about being restored, if I never lost my place, what would I know about His mercy if I hadn't gotten out of grace".* You see, being restored helps you to realize that you are in the wrong place and need mercy and grace to bring you back in. Restoration allows you to experience this grace and mercy and to know that no matter how far away you slip, God's love for you is always able to bring you back to Him. He never stops loving you and never stops wanting you to do what's right. God always wants you on His team and His unconditional love proves that He will always be there.

Hurting People Hurt People, But God HEALS ALL Wounds…

DeMarco was hurting from a very young age. He had seen things that no little boy should ever see. Losing his mother, father and grandmother made him become very rebellious. He expressed this anger in any way that he could. Everyone doesn't know how to express their feelings in healthy ways. This is why there are shootings and killings between people that say they love one another or people that feel that this is the way to express hate. If you do not learn self-control and allow God to control your life, you will handle things in a way that will hurt others. After DeMarco was in jail, he was able to detox from wrongful thoughts and see the things that he was doing wrong.

Unfortunately, everyone doesn't come out with DeMarco's story. Some leave jail only to go out and do the same thing or something worse. The good thing about DeMarco is that he had a foundation that allowed him to have something to think about. Proverbs 22:6 says: "***Point your kids in the right direction and when they are old they won't be lost.***" (MSG) This is why it is so important for parents to train up their children and seek God for the plan that He has for them so that they can put them on the right path. God gave children to parents so that they would have stewards and guidance over them. Sad to say, some parents are the instrument that destroys the child. In this case, DeMarco had the prayers and rearing of his Grandmother and even when he was older he had something to reflect on that changed his life forever.

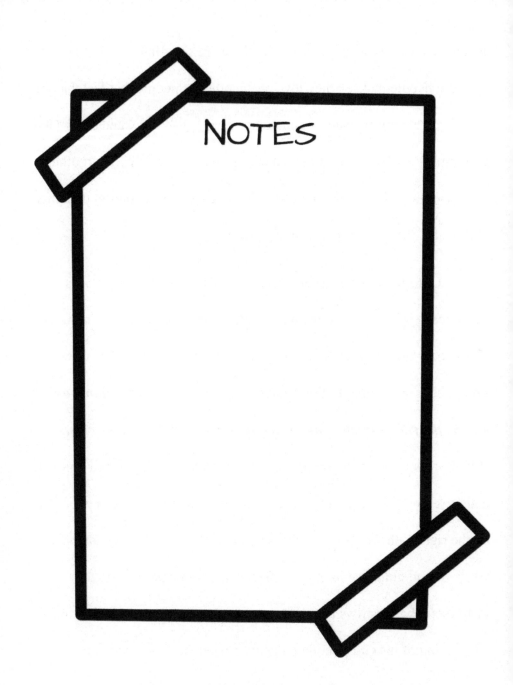

NOTES

Conclusion

Hurting people hurt people is about not judging people from the outside, but getting to know them through the spirit. What you see, can fool you because it may just be an imposter. It may affect us directly or indirectly. Some traumas may have lasting effects and some may not have any effect at all depending on the situation and the person. Nevertheless, in every case God is able to heal ALL wounds. Through the stories, I pray that you have learned some things that will help you along the way. From every life that we observe or experience, there are lessons to learn. Take a moment to identify what I've learned.

Jesus came, died and was crucified so that I might have an abundant life. I don't have to allow the enemy to take my goods. (John 10:10) therefore, I will no longer give him the consent to rape me of what God has given me. God foreknew me and has predestined me and He has a plan for my life (Romans 8:29), but it's up to me to seek Him to find my purpose. Forgiveness is a major part of healing. (Mark 11:25, ESV) It does not always mean reconciliation and it also doesn't let the other person off the hook. However, forgiveness does free you of the other person having control over you for the rest of your life.

Sometimes people don't even know that they have hurt you, especially if you don't tell them and sometimes they don't mean to hurt you, they are just hurting from the pain of someone else. I belong to God and although the enemy will try to make me feel less than, God always wants me to feel greater than. (I John 4:4) I am more than a conqueror (Romans 8:37) and no weapon that is formed against me shall prosper. (Isaiah 54:17) When all others forsake me, God will never leave me nor forsake me, but will always be with me. (Hebrews 13:5) Know that there is no condemnation to those that belong to Christ. (Romans 8:1, NLT)

The things that have happened to you do not make you who you are. God made you who He wanted you to be and you become stronger by learning how to handle the trials that come in your life. Everyone is not born privileged so you have to live the life that has been chosen for you and try your best to respond positively to each encounter that takes place. That's not to say that you will deal with everything properly, if you could do that, you wouldn't need God. He has given us the Holy Spirit to be our guide and to help us along the way. (John 16:13, NASB) Don't stay down no matter what happens to you, you can always bounce back as long as you don't give up.

Sometimes that may even mean you have to encourage yourself (I Samuel 30:6) because there is not always going to be someone there to do it for you. As for me, I have finally learned to accept death as a part of life and I realize that none of us can avoid it. As they say, "We're not getting out of here alive". Over the years, I have had to allow God to slowly help me to look at this from a different perspective. I also now understand that the reason that I couldn't deal with death was because I didn't know how to deal with life.

Nevertheless, as I began to ask myself what was most difficult for me when I thought about death and I found that it was the fear of the unknown, but when I had another one of my "uh oh" moments, I realized that we live in the unknown every day. Many of us are afraid of what we don't know about when we leave this place that we are so familiar with. Yes, we know that the bible tells us that God has prepared a place for us and we hear about how beautiful it will be, but we have no frame of reference except what we have read and what we believe.

Funny thing is that before we came to earth, we didn't have a frame of reference either, we just didn't know what we didn't know. But this is one thing I know for sure that we are spiritual beings having an earthly experience and if I believe and trust in God, He is in control. All I have to do is live according to His word, trust Him and know that He will always be with me. Psalm 139:8 says: *"If I ascend up into heaven, thou art there: if I make my bed in hell, behold, thou art there."*

Now, if you see yourself in any of these stories and are being affected negatively, ask God to change your perspective so that He can heal you. Ask Him to give you spiritual eyesight so that you are able to see where the enemy wants to keep you stuck. Ask Him to heal your wounds so that you only see the scars that prove you made it through the battle. Everybody is going through something, been through something or is getting ready to go through something. Therefore, we should treat everyone kindly because you don't know where they are in their process.

Remember what you see on the outside may not be the real person on the inside, you may just be seeing the fig leaves that they are using to cover all their pain. I'll leave you to have your own experience, but remember people are not just hurting people because they have been hurt in the past, they are also *hurting* people because they are still hurting in the present. We are bandaging the wounds, but not getting healed because we don't know how to add the negatives with the positives.

Restoration began for me at a time that most in the world was at a standstill. It was a turning point for the world and forced many to make decisions that they had been avoiding for many years. I had become content with the way things were because I could stay busy. Not always doing what God wanted me to do, not even always doing what I wanted to do. I realized that I always avoided being still because I didn't want to think. I realized that I was avoiding quiet time and often drowned out the voice of God because I always wanted to be busy so as to not take the time to think about my life and the many things that had taken place in it. But in drowning my life with the noise, I was also drowning out my dreams.

I had forgotten the many things that I once wanted to do in life and allowed myself to focus on others rather than to focus on what God had put inside of me. It seemed like as long as I could please others, I thought I was pleased, but I also realized that in pleasing others, God was not always pleased with me. During the pandemic, I couldn't focus on pleasing people because sometimes we weren't even able to see other people and I had to learn to live with myself. Now I will tell you, this moment was a battle for me because I hated being alone. In times past, I always made sure I was around people to avoid the quietness.

Imagine the surprise when I realized that I really enjoyed spending time with God and myself. I began to settle my mind and was able to reflect on how good God had really been to me. I was able to see how He had kept me from the things that the devil wanted to use to cause my demise. With these thoughts came a heart of gratefulness. I was able to see where the enemy should have won, but God blocked his plan. I was also able to see where my life should have been destroyed because of poor decisions, but God allowed the forces of grace and mercy to intervene. I was able to see how the enemy came to kill, steal and destroy, BUT God, came to give me life and that more abundantly. In this, I realized that the enemy didn't want me to take the time to quiet myself because as long as I couldn't see God's blessings and plans for my life, he could make me focus on all the things that I thought went wrong in my life, instead of all the places that God was present in my life.

Not long after the death of my husband, God gave me (Isaiah 54:4-6) as He told Israel. I knew He was telling me that He would be my Husband and would take care of me as He began immediately. But because of the hurt and pain that was on the inside, I honestly thought for all these years that God was setting me up to fail and I was falsely accusing Him. I never even thought that I would live to see my life get to this point. He could have taken me out and I could have died with a corrupt heart against God, but instead He had mercy. I was able to repent and ask God to forgive me and that's the place that restoration began.

I began to fill myself with positive thoughts and affirmations that tell me that I could, instead of the negative thoughts that would come first thing in the morning to regret the day and tell me that I can't. Restoration has allowed me to live and not just survive. I have grown leaps and bounds in my spiritual walk and thank God for where He now has my feet planted. Being restored has allowed me to enjoy life instead of regretting the day I was born. It has allowed me to dream again and look forward to the future, instead of always wondering how or when I was going to die.

I won't say that difficult times still don't present themselves, but I will say that now, every day I wake up grateful and I thank God for the ability to choose life. I now know that I am fearfully and wonderfully made (Psalm 139:14) and that I can do all things through Christ that strengthens me (Philippians 4:13), if I only trust Him. He told me to never forget my destiny and to never forget my dreams. He has brought new life and I'm grateful for what He has done and what He has in store. The best is yet to come!

From The Author's Desk

On Sept 10, 2000, I married my best friend and thought that we

would be together for many years to come. We started a life together, had

a beautiful baby girl, bought a house and things looked really positive. As

a matter of fact, it looked like the beginning of something great. But after

10 years of marriage, life changed drastically and I not only lost my

husband, but I also lost myself and was holding on the best I could not to

lose my mind. His work was done and I was left to raise an eight-year-old

all by myself. I definitely didn't see that coming and that's not how things

were supposed to turn out, well at least that's what I thought. I remember

being so angry with God because in my mind I thought that I had done

things the right way. I even argued with God about how I waited 35 years

to have a family and still ended up being a single parent.

Aren't you supposed to get married and then have a child to live

forever in bliss? Well at least that's the order I thought the bible told me.

When I finally came to my senses, I thought, "How self-righteous of

me?" the Bible says in Matthew 5:45 *"so that you may [show yourselves*

to] be the children of your Father who is in heaven; for He makes His

sun rise on those who are evil an on those who are good, and makes the rain fall on the righteous [those who are morally upright] and the unrighteous [the unrepentant, those who oppose Him]. (AMP) and besides, who said I was doing it right just because I did that one in the order that God commanded? But see, this was all from my perspective and what I thought life was supposed to be. It was about what I had planned and not what God had planned for me.

Although it may have seemed strange to some, I chose September 10, 2022 to rebrand and celebrate me. I was able to live and love my best friend for 10 years; the past eleven years, I've tried to learn to be the best single mom that I could be, while struggling through my own stuff. I left my previous church and yes, I was also mad with God about that. After this experience, I had decided in my mind to be done with church forever, but God used my daughter with a desire to attend another one.

So I thought I would try one more time for the sake of my child. It took me a long time to look at things from a different perspective and even see how God could be working things out for my good. So, as you see, I didn't have good thoughts about God most of the time either. I didn't think any good would come out of my life. I was pretty much just praying that God would allow me to stay around until my daughter turned 18 so that she was not disappointed with the loss of another parent.

I thought that God was setting me up for failure and I lost myself somewhere in the process. Even in the midst of all this God allowed me to choose me. He told me to "Never to Forget my Destiny and to Never Forget my Dreams" so I began to dream again. God has been teaching me that He is able to take care of me and do exceedingly and abundantly above all that I could ever ask or think. in 1 Peter 5:10, it says *"After you have suffered for a little while, the God of all grace [who imparts His blessing and favor], who called you to His own eternal glory in Christ, will Himself complete, confirm, strengthen, and establish you [making you what you ought to be].*

You see, while I was busy looking at one perspective from the outer appearance, God was doing something far greater on the inside from another perspective. I was showing up for others, but feeling pain, despair, and hopelessness on the inside. What I didn't understand was that He was turning every negative into a positive. He was doing what He said in Joel 2:25 *"And I will restore to you the years that the locust hath eaten…"* For the past few years, He has shown me that He will be my husband as He told me in the beginning and even in the midst of all the chaos that's going on in the world, I've learned to trust God.

I've celebrated almost 14 years on a job that I never thought that I was qualified for. I've had the pleasure of watching my daughter blossom and now become a junior in college. I've watched this book come to fruition, which I definitely never saw in my future. I've been a part of a loving and supportive church with extended family and friends that love me and not just tolerate me. Through this process, although He used the government to manifest it, I will always know that it was God who allowed my student loans to be forgiven (this alone, showed me His grace). For those who know me, know that I had made a career out of going to school and I loved to learn and I shall return.

By the grace of God, I was able to pay off my car and I will soon be debt free to purchase a home *(something else that I no longer wanted because I associated it with pain).* So yes, moving forward, I choose God and I choose to celebrate all that He has done for me. After reading this book, I pray that you too will focus on the positive and not the negative as you speak those things that you want in your life.

"As it is written…..-the God who gives life to the dead and calls into being things that were not." (Romans 4:17 NIV)

Never Forget Your Destiny

By Neet Frazier-Diggs

Never forget your destiny,

Never forget your dreams!

Life has many twists and turns,

it's not always what it seems.

You live your life, you do your best,

sometimes forgetting that life's just a test;

a course of decisions you must learn to make,

many ups and downs and lots of mistakes.

But God has a purpose, He knows why you're here

if you don't trust Him, you'll live in the midst of your fears.

From the womb of your mother, He predestined your life,

He has plans of good, not evil, not misery or strife,

You see the work God began, He wants to complete,

teach you how to be triumphant and put the devil under your feet.

Key is you must seek him for purpose for this plan to come through,

So He can bring out those things that may be hiding in you,

It may not be easy, but it will come together as it should,

Remember, it's a promise, He's working it out for your good.

So never forget your destiny and never forget your dreams,

but Trust in your Heavenly Father, who sent His Son to redeem.

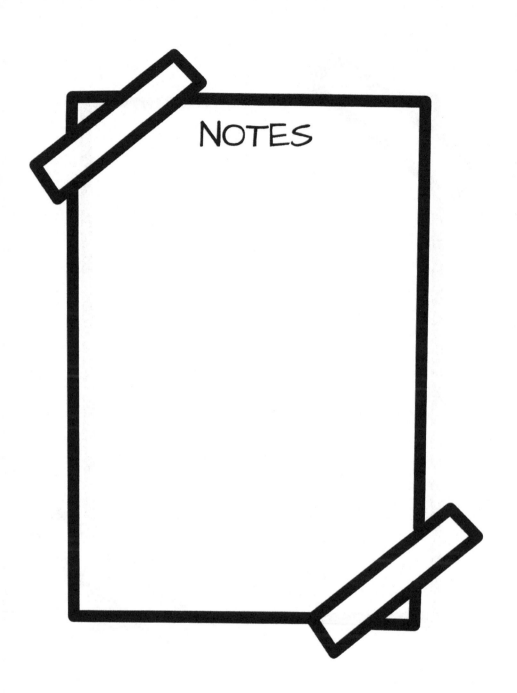

NOTES

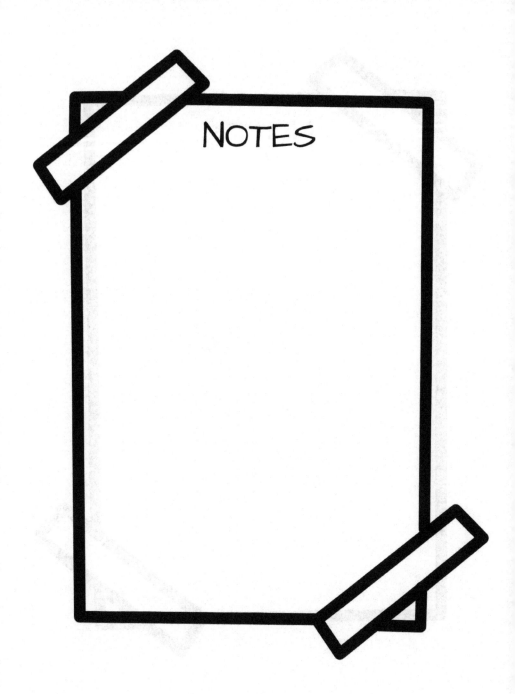

NOTES

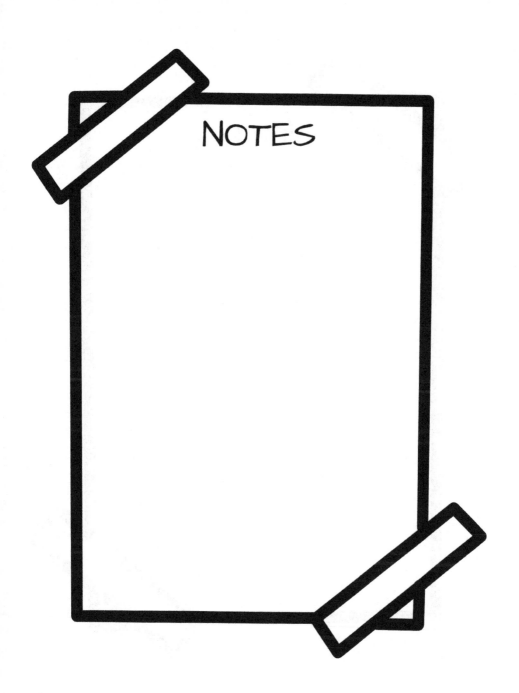

NOTES

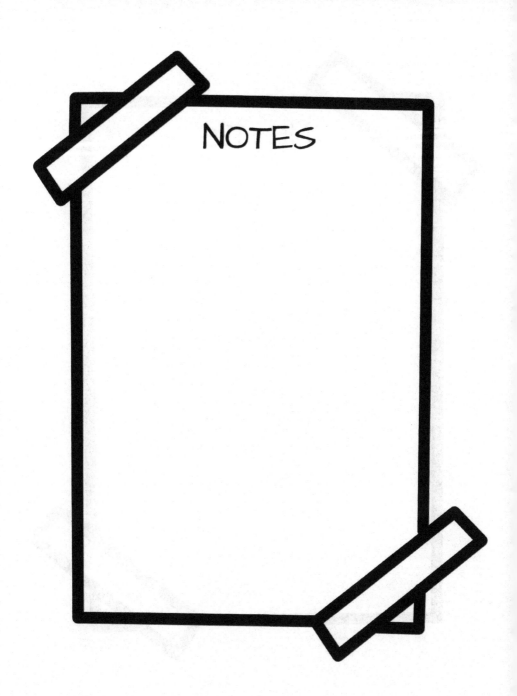

NOTES

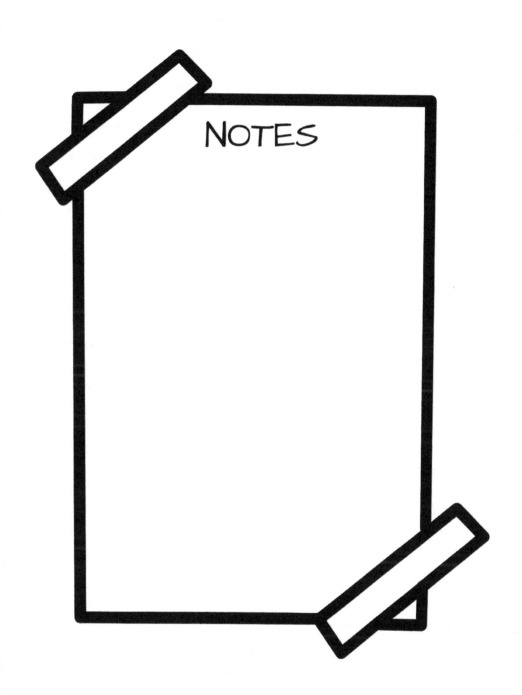

NOTES

This labor of love and faith was years in the making. Throughout this journey there were some musical selections that guided me along my way from start to finish. You may view the entire playlist below or scan this QR code to listen to my inspirational music playlist of songs. Prayerfully, they will motivate you for better days.

I do not own the rights to this music.

New York Restoration (Speak to my heart) -
https://youtu.be/t0roQR42MPo
Smokie Norful (I Understand) - https://youtu.be/l0skD7d3usw
Tasha Cobbs (In spite of me) - https://youtu.be/gE15aoHyIl8
Lamont Sanders (He Kept Me) - https://youtu.be/DzlpuobmeN8
James Fortune (Hold On) - https://youtu.be/6TYP_1Zibu4
Travis Greene (He's Intentional) - https://youtu.be/Fb2wNc1Owpc
Tamela Mann (He Did It for Me) - https://youtu.be/3yz0iQID6yQ
JJ Hairston (Thankful) - https://youtu.be/p9iN1rYT0K8
Zacardi Cortez You've Been Good to Me –
https://youtu.be/_dEWFGEHiY0
Kingdom (Fully Committed) - https://youtu.be/qCV6kZY4Pv4
Fred Jerkins (Walking in Victory) https://youtu.be/15NwKEueJzg
Erica Campbell (Positive) - https://youtu.be/_XBGhhdEuzA
Upper Room (Surrounded) – https://youtu.be/nWmjpF613y4

About The Author

Neet Frazier-Diggs is a native of Chestertown, Maryland, but was raised in Havre De Grace, Maryland from the age of nine. After receiving her high school education, she embarked upon an opportunity to travel to Germany. She lived in Germany for three years before her return to MD however she eventually settled in Georgia. Neet successfully earned her B.S. degree in Telecommunications and later received her M.S. degree in Computer Science. She also holds a Certificate in Accounting and Bookkeeping. Neet has served professionally as a Project Administrator, Network Specialist, and Business Manager. Despite these accolades her faith remained of the utmost importance. As a young girl, Neet began working in ministry at Evangelistic Church of Deliverance under the leadership of her grandmother, the late Pastor Patricia Pringle. In 1997, she became a licensed Minister. She later joined Love Divine Family Worship Center, under the leadership of the late Dr. Stanley Diggs. Neet served at LDFWC for fourteen years in the capacity of the first church Secretary, Director of Finance, Praise & Worship Leader, Youth Director, and Minister. Neet now attends Set The Captives Free Outreach Center (STCFOC) under the leadership of Pastors Karen and Linwood Bethea.

On September 10, 2000, Neet entered wedded bliss with Michael Diggs. The two were together until his untimely passing in 2011. Their union produced a loving daughter, MaLeah Diggs. Despite her grief and loss, Neet continued to be a multifaceted and creative individual. While enjoying her graphic design and balloon art talents, she started her own company known as Uneek Designs. From there, God ordered her steps towards becoming an author and birthed her new book: *"Hurting People Hurt People, But God Heals All Wounds"*. This book views our outward appearances while trying to understand our inward struggles. In 1 Samuel 16:7, the Lord says: *"**man looks on the outward appearance, but the Lord looks on the heart.**"* Her debut book takes a look at the problem and the solution from different perspectives while showing how the outcomes can be different based on our choices in life. In her spare time, Neet enjoys spending time with family and friends, traveling, and serving in her church. She has also found herself coaching high school girls' basketball and working with adults with developmental disabilities. She believes wholeheartedly in Ecclesiastes 9:10, which says *"**whatever thy hand findeth to do, do it with thy might**"*.

Made in the USA
Columbia, SC
21 October 2022